THE BOOK IN ROOM 316

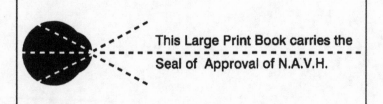

This Large Print Book carries the
Seal of Approval of N.A.V.H.

THE BOOK IN ROOM 316

RESHONDA TATE BILLINGSLEY

THORNDIKE PRESS
A part of Gale, a Cengage Company

Farmington Hills, Mich • San Francisco • New York • Waterville, Maine
Meriden, Conn • Mason, Ohio • Chicago

Copyright © 2018 by ReShonda Tate Billingsley.
Thorndike Press, a part of Gale, a Cengage Company.

Thorndike Press® Large Print African-American.
The text of this Large Print edition is unabridged.
Other aspects of the book may vary from the original edition.
Set in 16 pt. Plantin.

LIBRARY OF CONGRESS CIP DATA ON FILE.
CATALOGUING IN PUBLICATION FOR THIS BOOK
IS AVAILABLE FROM THE LIBRARY OF CONGRESS

ISBN-13: 978-1-4328-5565-9 (hardcover)

Published in 2018 by arrangement with Gallery Books, an imprint of Simon & Schuster, Inc.

Printed in Mexico
1 2 3 4 5 6 7 22 21 20 19 18

For E.B.

SAVANNAH

CHAPTER 1

For better or for worse.

That was such a load of crap. Surely, those words were written by some polygamous man who wanted all the trappings with a wife and the dalliances with a mistress.

A sea of thoughts swirled through my head as I recalled my wedding vows — vows that I'd faithfully upheld for the past twelve years.

Do you, Savannah Dionne Kirby, take this man . . .

Vows I'd been foolish enough to believe my husband, Clark, had upheld as well.

Do you, Clark Edward Graham, take this woman . . .

Vows that, 4,603 days after I'd made them, didn't mean a single thing.

"Can I get anything else for you?"

The bartender's chipper voice forced me out of my wedding-day memories and into my present-day nightmare. I swallowed the lump in my throat, forced a smile, and said, "May I have another, please?"

He kept his smile as his left eyebrow rose in judgment. "You sure about that?"

My right eyebrow rose to let him know I wasn't in the mood to be judged. "Look, I just need a gin and Coke. I don't need a shot of lecture."

He shrugged, then went to make my drink. My eyes stayed on his backside as he walked away.

I couldn't remember the last time that I'd let my eyes roam over another man. When it came to faithfulness, I could've been the spokesperson for the Committed Wives Society.

Not anymore.

"It's not often I see a woman going for hard liquor like that."

I turned toward the stranger who had sat on the bar stool next to mine and slid into my thoughts as if I had summoned him up. Even though he was sitting, he had to be at least six-four. With a smile that looked like it should be hawking teeth-whitening products, this man's rugged good looks were made for a magazine cover. He looked like a black George Clooney in his tan blazer and dark denim jeans, which gave off the perfect combination of a business-casual vibe. He was the absolute total package. And all I could think was that he was invading my personal space.

"Mind if I sit?" he asked, setting his half-empty glass on the bar.

I exhaled, let my shoulders slump in exasperation, then turned back to face forward. "You're already sitting."

"Mind if I sit *here*?" he corrected. He pulled some cash out and set it on the bar. "And I would love to buy you that gin and Coke."

My first reaction was to do what I'd always done when men approached me — which was quite often thanks to my voluptuous figure and smooth caramel skin that screamed twenty-nine instead of my actual thirty-eight, and kept me working as one of the most popular TV reporters in town when most of my female colleagues the same age had moved on to another career. But before I could utter the words "I'm married," another thought filled my head: Clark didn't care about being married.

Clark.

The reason I was sitting in the bar at the Markham Hotel in downtown Houston, drowning my sorrows in my third glass of gin and Coke.

I didn't even drink gin and Coke.

"How do you know what I'm drinking anyway? Are you watching me?" I asked, shaking off thoughts of my husband.

"I wasn't watching you, but I definitely noticed you," he replied, not at all intimidated by the barb behind my words. I rolled my eyes and he shifted uncomfortably, like he was debating whether he should get up and leave or keep trying to talk to me. "This weather is a beast." He pointed toward the floor-to-ceiling window, at the pounding rain assaulting the pavement outside the hotel. It had started pouring down when I'd arrived at the hotel ten hours ago. I told myself it was the angels mixing their tears with mine.

"I'm from Dallas and was going to try to head home, but the weather is even worse there," the man continued. "It's flooding pretty bad, so I figured I'd just leave tomorrow. The only problem is that means I'm missing my daughter's recital. So, I've just been sitting over there, nursing my own sorrows."

I wondered why he thought I wanted to know his life story. But I just said, "Who said I'm nursing sorrows?" My voice was filled with attitude with this man who hadn't been invited to my pity party — however gorgeous he was.

He smiled as he raised his drink to his lips. "I know the eyes of a woman who's been hurt."

That made my heart ache and broke down my tough facade. As if I could possibly feel any more pain than what I'd felt ten hours ago when I'd overheard Clark's conversation with Dawn.

My good friend Dawn, the wife of Clark's late best friend.

I blinked back my welling tears — I'd shed enough of those — just as the bartender set my drink in front of me. The liquor was a welcome reprieve, and I quickly took a gulp.

"This is just what I need," I said, raising the glass in a mock toast. "Matter of fact, this is all I need to wipe away any sorrow." I winced, both from the liquor and the budding headache. I shook it off, reminded myself that I wasn't a weakling, then had to close my eyes as I got my bearings.

When I opened my eyes, my new neighbor was just staring at me with a smile that bore no judgment. Instead, I saw understanding in his eyes.

"I'm Wilson," he said, extending his hand.

"You have a last name for a first name?" I giggled, my guard slightly lowering thanks to the mixture of gin and revenge.

He shrugged. "My mother always had to

be different. And you are?"

I hesitated, allowing Clark and Dawn a millisecond to creep back into my thoughts.

I silently cursed my husband and my friend and said, "I'm Savannah. Savannah Graham."

Dang it, I immediately thought. I should've given him my maiden name, since I'd be returning to it soon. Or better yet, a fake name. If he was from Dallas, he wouldn't have known me from television anyway.

"I'm a good listener," Wilson said. It was as if he knew that I was fighting off the worst kind of pain.

Usually, there was no way in the world I would've shared my private business with a complete stranger. But the last ten hours had been the stuff nightmares were made of. And if this handsome stranger could help me pick up the pieces of my broken heart, then so be it.

I shrugged. "Hey, it's the usual story behind a woman sitting in a bar alone, drowning her sorrows in liquor. I just found out the man I thought would love me forever is loving on another woman."

Images of Clark and Dawn once again filled my head. Every time they'd laughed. Every time they'd spoken. I was now trying to dissect every memory.

"Wow, sorry to hear that," Wilson said.

I took another sip of my drink, then grimaced as the liquor burned my throat as it went down. "It is what it is. Now I just have to figure out how to move on."

"Yeah. I'm divorced myself. It wasn't easy, especially on my kids. Do you have children?" Wilson asked.

That brought another pang to my heart. Maybe that's why Clark had slept with Dawn. I had been unable to give him the one thing he wanted most. Dawn, on the other hand, had four kids. So, of course, he'd end up in the arms of the most fertile woman on the planet.

"No. No kids," I said. "We were in the process of trying to adopt, but there have been all kinds of delays. I guess that was God's way of keeping that from happening." I released a pained laugh. I had to laugh, so I didn't cry.

"I really am sorry." Concern had replaced his gorgeous smile.

I paused and composed myself before this man thought I was a nut job.

Wilson placed his hand on my arm. "I hate to see a beautiful woman like you going through something like this."

A jolt of electricity shot through me at his touch. It had been thirteen years since another man had electrified me like this. Thirteen years since I'd even desired anyone other than Clark.

Betrayal had a way of quickly changing things. And since I was now doing things I'd never before done, maybe I should go all the way. Maybe I should give Clark a taste of his own medicine. Maybe Wilson could help fill the hole in my heart.

"You know, I don't want to talk about that anymore," I abruptly said, brushing down my rose pencil skirt and turning to face him. "My marriage is finished and I just want to have a good time enjoying my drink, then go back to my room and drink some more."

Wilson's eyes instinctively noticed my toned legs, then traveled back up my body, until we were both exchanging hungry glances. He licked his lips, desire filling his eyes. "I have a bottle of Grey Goose in my room. I could grab it and meet you back in your room to, ah, talk, or whatever you'd like to do."

Any other time, the thought of going to a hotel room with any man other than Clark would've mortified me. But this wasn't any other time.

Clark had betrayed me.

An eye for an eye.

"You know, that sounds like an excellent

idea," I said. The liquid courage had given me juice, and I stood before I came to my senses.

"Room 316," I whispered. "See you soon."

I ran my hand along his chest, then sauntered toward the elevator knowing his eyes were following me and taking comfort in the fact that I was about to give my husband the payback he deserved.

CHAPTER 2

Forsaking all others . . .

I squeezed my eyes closed, trying to push aside the voice raging in my head. I needed to erase the image of Clark and Dawn that was on constant replay in my mind. I needed to forget the hushed tone of them discussing their affair. I needed to forget how I'd overheard them when I'd left the mayhem of the television newsroom and popped up at Dawn's house in the middle of the day, to surprise her teenaged daughter with tickets to see Bryson Tiller.

Only I was the one surprised.

I don't want to hurt her, he'd said.

I never meant for this to happen, she'd replied.

Liars! Both of them.

I paced my hotel room for a moment. I'd raced here to the Markham, seeking refuge from the pain of betrayal, and had told the front desk clerk that I'd be here a few days.

18

Though the more I thought about it, the more I felt like I could never go home again.

I glanced over at my overnight bag that I'd stuffed some belongings into before I'd fled our house. I considered it a house now because Clark's betrayal meant it was no longer a home.

I needed to change out of the business clothes I'd been wearing, put on the maxi dress that I'd packed, then put away thoughts of the pain.

And right now, Wilson was the best medicine for what ailed me.

The incessant tears hadn't worked.

The liquor hadn't worked.

Maybe this would.

My reflection stopped my thoughts. My eyes were reddening — from the liquor and the tears.

"Suck it up," I muttered. "You're stronger than this."

I had just slipped on the hunter-green dress that hugged my figure in all the right places when I heard a tap on the door.

I ran my fingers through my curls, checked the mirror to make sure my reflection didn't reveal my ache, then headed to the door.

"Hey," I said, swinging the door open and seductively leaning against the frame.

"My God, you're so beautiful," Wilson

said as if he were seeing me for the first time.

I smiled, then stepped aside for him to enter.

I offer my solemn vow to be a faithful partner . . .

I cursed the righteous voice invading my seduction. All signs pointed toward this; it was what I needed to help me heal. And I needed to get down to business before the voice overpowered me, brought me back to the woman I was before Clark's infidelity.

Wilson set the bottle of Grey Goose down on the desk. "So, how do you like your drink?"

I didn't reply. I wasn't interested in small talk. I just wanted to forget. I wanted to hurt Clark like he'd hurt me.

"Tall, dark, and handsome," I said, gliding over to him.

My boldness as I began removing his blazer must have been intoxicating enough because he quickly forgot about the liquor and let my hands roam his body.

"Mmmmm." Wilson closed his eyes and moaned as I ran my hands under his shirt and caressed his chest. "I like that."

I removed his blazer and shirt and massaged his chest, my hands exploring every muscular inch, the intensity of my exploration rising with every moan.

"Oooh, that feels so good," he said, reaching down and lifting my dress as his hands moved over my thighs.

Fueled by the gin, driven by revenge, I all but ripped Wilson's shirt off.

I will love and cherish . . .

Why wouldn't that voice leave me alone? I deserved this. Clark deserved to pay. I didn't need the verbal torture playing out in my head.

Our lips met, and Wilson guided us toward the foot of the bed, then gently pushed me down, while he moaned in pleasure.

"I can't wait to feel you . . ." His voice was husky, his desire palpable as he climbed on top of me.

"Owww," I said, squirming as something poked me in the back. I reached behind me, under the duvet that had been draped across the foot of the bed, and pulled out what appeared to be a tattered book.

"What is that?" Wilson asked, pausing as he took the book from my hand. "Wow. Talk about a buzz killer." He turned the book around so it faced me.

Though flakes of the gold enamel lettering were missing, the word "Bible" was etched across the front.

My eyes widened in shock. Yet an unfazed

Wilson deftly moved over to the nightstand and set the book down.

"Now, where were we?" He crawled back on the bed and resumed nuzzling my neck.

And hereto I pledge you my faithfulness.

The words both Clark and I had pledged before family and friends on that beautiful August day took their place at the forefront of my mind.

What in the world was I doing?

Had I really been about to make love to another man on top of a Bible?

Wilson's labored breathing brought me out of my thoughts.

"Stop," I said. "I-I can't do this." I squirmed from under him and scooted to the edge of the bed.

Frustration filled Wilson's face as he sat up next to me, and a tinge of fear filled my heart. I didn't know anything about this man. He could be a rapist or a murderer, and I'd opened my door and let the devil in.

"I-I'm so sorry," I stammered as I stood up, putting some distance between us. "I don't know what I'm doing. My husband cheated, but I . . . This isn't me. I'm going through a rough time, and I'm not thinking clearly." I rushed my words out as I tried to shake off the lingering effects of the liquor.

I expected Wilson to protest, get angry, but instead he took a deep breath, in and out, then nodded in understanding.

"You don't have to explain. I get it."

He stood and adjusted himself. If he was upset, he wasn't showing it.

"You're a beautiful woman." He paused, and I realized that I didn't even know his last name. I was about to have sex with a man whose last name I didn't even know. "And I'm not going to lie," he continued, "I was looking forward to this. But no means no," he replied. He picked his shirt and blazer up off the floor and slipped the white button-down back on. "Your husband is a lucky man."

Those words brought tears to my eyes, but I blinked them back and willed them not to fall.

Wilson threw his blazer across his arm, then dug in his pants pocket. "Here's my card," he said, handing me his business card. "If things don't work out with your marriage, feel free to call me. Next time we'll just start with coffee."

I managed a smile as I took his card. Wilson Parsons. Now I had that at least. "Thank you" was all I could say.

Infidelity has caused me to take leave of common sense, I thought as he walked out the door. Thank God I'd encountered a decent man. Because this scenario could've ended very differently.

Till death do us part.

My gaze settled on the book that had brought me to my senses. I picked it up and ran my fingers over the rough cover. It was strange. This was definitely not the standard Gideon Bible placed in all hotel rooms. The frayed cover made the book appear to be decades old.

I plopped on the bed and flipped the book open. The pages were worn, as if the book had been passed down for generations. I had walked away from God five years ago when he hadn't fulfilled my prayer of motherhood, so I hadn't opened a Bible for a long time. *No need to start now,* I thought as I tossed the book back onto the nightstand. Yes, it had kept me from making a horrible mistake, but it hadn't changed my situation.

The book teetered on the edge of the nightstand, then fell to the floor, opening to reveal a tattered page.

Ashamed of my carelessness, I leaned down to pick it up. Before I could close the Bible, the verse that the book had opened to caught my eye.

Psalm 147:3 — He healeth the broken in

heart, and bindeth up their wounds.

The verse made my heart drop. It was the same one that Clark had repeated when he brought me back from the depths of despair.

That verse — and my husband — had saved my life.

Chapter 3

September 2010

My wounds could not be healed. The therapist had not been able to do it. My best friend, Yvonne, had not been able to do it. Nor could my beloved Clark.

Nothing could bring me out of the black hole of grief.

I didn't know how long it had been since I'd uttered a word. Death had a way of silencing people. And I had been comfortable settling into the pit of despair. The only voice I'd been able to find was the one praying for God to take me in my sleep. If I wasn't such a coward, I would've downed a bottle of pills and given God some assistance.

"Look, you have to move past this."

Yvonne's voice shook me out of my self-induced trance. My best friend since middle school had been by my side almost as much as Clark. Only unlike his, Yvonne's tone had changed from concern to exasperation.

26

"It has been six months, Savannah," Yvonne said, reaching up to tie her long, curly hair into a ponytail, like she needed to get comfortable to knock some sense into me. "I know this is hard, but you've got to come back. You've got to shake off this grief."

How do you shake off grief? I screamed inside. *How do you get rid of the never-ending sound of your mother's cry that haunts you? A cry that she emitted as she lay dying in your arms from an accident that you caused?*

Who gets over that?

A text. A stupid text about a story I was trying to scoop the competition on. A text that just couldn't wait and had killed my mother, my unborn child, and my future children . . . and left me to deal with the aftermath.

No, I had no interest in coming back from that. I was going to stay in my fallen state forever.

Yvonne scooted next to me on the sofa — my permanent place of residence since I'd come home after six weeks in the hospital and rehab to heal a broken leg.

I'd merely broken my leg.

The deaths of my mother and baby had broken my heart. And yet I got to come home.

The guilt had driven me into an abyss of darkness. There was no light in my life. I was cloaked in grief, and it permeated everything I did. Or didn't do. The weight of knowing I'd killed my mother, my child, and my womb had left me unable to function, and the sofa had become my refuge. I spent my days and nights in alternate states of depression, tears, and sadness. Now, as Yvonne wiped tears that constantly appeared without warning, I wondered if I'd ever see light again.

"Sweetie, I want to help you," she said, her expression a mixture of worry and irritation. "We all want to help. But you have to open up and let us in."

I pulled the afghan more tightly around me. I'd vowed that all I'd do for the rest of my life was exactly what I'd been doing for the past four months — sit on this sofa and wait to die.

"Clark lost his child. He can't lose you, too." Yvonne then said what she always said. "He's a good guy, one of the best. But there's only so much any man can take when his wife shuts him out. You have to come back — for Clark. Before he leaves," she added.

"I'm not going anywhere."

The sight of Clark standing in the entryway, the sunlight capturing his profile, showering him with the aura of a Wakandan king, made my heart flutter. I loved my husband so much, but love wasn't enough to save me.

Clark walked over to the sofa, sat on the other side of me, and took my hand.

"No matter how long it takes, I'm going to love my wife and help her past this pain." He lifted my chin and gazed into my eyes as he continued. "I'm going to do whatever it takes. We will deal with this grief together. The Lord heals the brokenhearted and binds up their wounds."

I snuggled into his embrace. Though I wasn't responding, I heard his prayer. It was how he ended every night as he tucked me into my spot on the sofa. Clark was the religious one in our marriage. He'd been raised in one of those Sunday-through-Sunday church-going Baptist homes. The foundation his mother and grandmother had laid ran deep. I was more spiritual than religious. But ever since I'd overheard his mother complaining that we were unequally yoked, back when we first started dating, I'd tried to channel my husband's faith.

It had worked, too. I had happily opened the door to religion. But now — after this — I'd slammed that bad boy shut.

"I'm gonna go," Yvonne said. "I gotta go check on my parents. You know my mom hasn't been feeling well. And my hypochondriac sister has diagnosed her based off something she read on the Internet." She leaned over and kissed me on top of my head, then squeezed Clark's hand. "Thank you so much. I'm so glad she has you."

I nestled closer to my husband, my back resting against his chest. As I watched Yvonne leave, Clark's hands instinctively went to my stomach and I tensed. I hated for him to touch the home of the child we would never know.

As if reading my thoughts, he whispered, "You know it's not your fault. I don't blame you."

How could he not? The crushed metal from my car had pierced my amniotic sac — and my womb — ensuring that he would never have the children he so desperately wanted.

"We are going to get through this together," he said, holding me tighter. "I'm here for you till death do us part."

I didn't realize I was crying as I sat on the edge of the hotel bed. At the time, I'd felt that Clark deserved so much more than what I had been giving him. He had suffered through my grief and loved me out of it. It had taken another six weeks, but his love had given me a will to live.

I slapped my face as I wiped the tears brought on by that memory. I was supposed to be angry, vengeful. Why was I thinking about the good part of my marriage? All of that had been ruined because Clark slept with another woman. So much for his religion.

I snarled at the book, before slamming it shut.

This Bible was bringing back things I didn't want to remember. All I wanted to think about was how the two people I cared about most had broken my heart.

The Lord heals the brokenhearted and binds up their wounds.

"Ugh," I groaned, tossing the Bible on the bed as I stood. An eerie feeling swept over me as the book fell open again . . . and back to Psalm 147:3.

I looked around the room as if some supernatural force was at play. My eyes drifted back to the book — and the tattered pages. The pages fluttered, despite the fact that there was no breeze.

"No," I said, picking the book up and slamming it shut again, before setting it on the desk. My mind was playing tricks on me. The gin and Cokes had taken their toll.

This book had stopped me from sleeping with a stranger, but that's it. Nothing more. If God was in this equation, He would've stopped Clark like He'd stopped me.

I fell back across the bed and cried myself to sleep.

CHAPTER 4

I had fallen asleep with betrayal on my mind. And I'd awakened with more thoughts of revenge. I groaned as my head throbbed from all the liquor that I'd consumed yesterday. I didn't drink like that, and that's why I was paying the price this morning.

A shower and some breakfast helped ease my hangover, and I knew it was time to figure out my next step. I needed to start with my cell phone. I'd cut it off yesterday after I called my boss and told her that I needed some personal days. Since she was a friend in addition to being my boss, she was sympathetic without probing.

I don't think my phone had ever been off for a solid twenty-four hours. I knew Clark was going crazy with worry, but right now, honestly, I didn't care. Even still, I picked my phone up off the nightstand and powered it on. Clark had probably called everyone under the sun looking for me. And I didn't want everyone else to worry about me.

As soon as the screen popped on, I saw the notification that my mailbox was full. I opened the messaging app and saw the urgent texts from Clark's work phone, because I'd blocked his cell phone number. And for every one text he sent, Yvonne had sent two more.

If you don't call me right now, the last text from her said.

I sighed and then dialed my best friend's number.

"Savannah! Are you dead?" she cried, answering without bothering to say hello.

"I'm fine," I said, taking a seat at the desk.

"Then you have lost your mind!" she barked. "Do you know how unbelievably worried we have been? We didn't know if you had been kidnapped by a serial killer, run into a tree, or what."

I could tell she immediately regretted her choice of words because of my accident. But I chose to ignore the reference. I couldn't be concerned with that now.

I understood that Yvonne was worried — her job as an ER nurse had her always thinking the worst no matter what. But this wasn't about her. Or Clark. Or anyone else who was worried. This was about me.

"Look, I'm going through a lot," I said. "And I'm just taking some time to get my head together."

"Where are you?" she asked. When I didn't reply, she repeated, "Savannah, where are you?"

Yvonne had always been like my big sister, and I knew there would be no taking no for an answer. She would call out the cavalry until she tracked me down.

So I just told her. "I'm at the Markham Hotel, but do not tell Clark."

"I'm not even talking to Clark. That jerk cheated on you, so he's on my list."

I was a little shocked that he had told her. I might not have understood the whys behind Clark's transgression, but I knew he would never want anyone — especially my overprotective best friend — to know what he had done.

"So you know?" I asked.

"Yeah, he called trying to see if you were with me. Then he tried to give me some cockamamie story about you just leaving, but I know you, and we both know you wouldn't have just taken off."

"I know, right?" I said.

"So, I pressed him until he came clean. And girl, despite what he did, I can tell you

34

he's a complete basket case of worry."

I rolled my eyes and said, "Good."

Yvonne finally exhaled a sigh of relief. "Well, look, I'm on my way over there."

"No, really, Yvonne. I need to be alone," I said.

"Oh, I'm sorry," she replied. "Did that sound like it had a question mark at the end? I didn't say, 'Can I come over there?' I said I'm on my way. Markham? That's the hotel downtown, right?"

I thought about protesting, then decided maybe talking to my best friend would help me sort through things, figure out my next move.

"Fine," I said. "I'm in Room 316." Then I thought about it. If I let Yvonne in here, she might never leave. "You know what? I'm hungry, so just meet me in the restaurant downstairs."

"Okay. I'm on my way."

The waiter had already served my New England clam chowder by the time Yvonne arrived. She hugged me like I'd been missing for months, even though I just saw her three days ago.

"You have no idea how worried I was," she said. "I called every hospital in a fifty-mile radius." Yvonne took a seat across from me, set her purse on the table, and crossed her arms. "Okay. So, start from the beginning and tell me what happened."

The waiter approached us. "Ma'am, can I get you something?"

"Not now." Yvonne's tone sent the waiter scurrying away.

She glared at me. "Get to talking."

"What has Clark told you?" I asked.

"That he messed up. That he hurt you. He's dying because he doesn't know where you are."

"Good," I said.

"Would you just tell me what happened?" she snapped.

It took me less than ten minutes to fill her in on everything. And by the time I was done, her arms had unfolded and her fists were balled up on the table. She looked like she was ready to go exact some punishment of her own on Clark.

"Clark and Dawn?" she finally muttered, still in awe.

I nodded.

Her surprise turned to sympathy. "I'm so sorry, Savannah."

I ran my finger around the rim of my water glass. "You and me both."

"That dirty little home wrecker," Yvonne said. By default, Dawn had become a good friend to her as well. Yvonne didn't get along with too many people, but she liked Dawn. "And here I thought she was your friend."

"You and me both," I repeated.

"You know I called the heifer."

I shook my head and managed a terse laugh. "I should've known. What did she say?"

"You know she didn't answer." She paused as her expression softened. "Savannah, are you sure you didn't misconstrue things? Maybe —"

The look on my face made her stop in the middle of her sentence.

"Yeah, you never have been one to over-react," she continued, "and Clark did confess that he had cheated on you with her." She released an exasperated sigh. "But why did they do it? What happened?"

"Does it matter?" I said. "I didn't stick around for an explanation."

The waiter stood back with my club sandwich in his hand. I smiled and motioned for him to set my food down, which he did. Then he turned to Yvonne again.

"Would you like anything?"

Thankfully, Yvonne smiled. "Sorry for being rude. Dealing with some heavy stuff. Just bring me an apple martini, please. I'm not eating."

The waiter nodded and took off.

"You know you need to leave him a big tip," I said.

She flicked off my comment. "Anyway, I don't think I've ever seen Clark so desperate."

I hesitated. "I can't believe Clark talked to you about it, to be honest."

"I mean, he told me, but only the overview. I could tell he wanted to explain himself, but his focus was on finding you." She took a deep breath, and I could feel some more of her anger dissipate. "Okay, Savannah, I'm going to say this and I want you to seriously consider it. I know this is an emotional time and you're ready to call a divorce attorney, but you do know that couples have come back from affairs before?"

Just hearing the word "divorce" made my heart constrict. I thought Clark and I were a forever couple. We'd both experienced our parents divorcing when we were young, and we'd been adamant that that would not be our destiny.

And yet divorce seemed like the only cure for my ailing heart.

"No, this is different," I said. "Maybe if I didn't know her. Maybe if she hadn't been in my house, broken bread with my family. I mean, for God's sake, Dawn has been there through this whole adoption process with us . . ." I buried my face in my hands. "Oh, my God. What does this mean for the adoption?"

I felt a pain as I thought of that. Clark and I had finally broken down and gone to an adoption agency after I got over the hurt of the miscarriage — and the fact that I'd never be able to have kids again. We had been on a waiting list for the past year, but they'd been confident that they would find us a child, especially because we were amenable to taking an older boy or girl. Maybe this was just the universe's way of keeping another child from coming into a broken home.

Yvonne put her hands over mine as if she knew where my thoughts were drifting.

"What's going to happen now is we're going to talk about this," she said, her voice gentle, trying to reason with me. She paused as the waiter approached, set her drink down, then slowly backed away. "I'm furious with Clark, but the two of you will work through this. You'll go to counseling. You'll curse him out, pull out some of Aunt Florence's made-up curse words," she said, bringing a smile to my face as I recalled my mother. She despised profanity, so she created her own cursing vocabulary.

"Then you'll cry," Yvonne continued, "tell Clark how much he hurt you. He'll apologize, and you'll eventually forgive him because in your heart you know he's a good guy who did a bad thing. And then the two of you can still move forward with the adoption."

I jerked my hands away because the last thing I felt like hearing was a "life goes on" speech. My husband had betrayed me in the worst possible way. And I didn't see how in the world I'd be able to move forward from that.

"Yvonne, there is no coming back from this," I said.

"Said every person who ever came back from something horrible." Yvonne sighed, like she knew it was going to be hard to get through to me. She took a sip of her drink then added, "Okay, let's talk about this. Why do you think they slept together?"

I cocked my head, trying to see if she was for real.

"Seriously? Does the why matter?"

"It does," she answered matter-of-factly. "Because if this was something calculated, something that they plotted and planned, then that's just evil. And we need to go grab

Torrey and his crew and roll up on both of them."

The mention of my convict cousin made me half-smile.

"But," she continued, "if this is something that just happened, well, that's a different story. Plotting and planning versus getting caught up in the moment is very different."

My mind went back to Wilson and what almost happened.

"No." I shook away that thought. With Wilson I was driven by revenge. Clark had no excuse. "Look," I told my best friend, "all I know is he cheated on me and I can't trust him ever again. How would we ever recover from that?"

"I don't know. But I do know it's possible. You can't let one bad thing wipe away all the good. And I know you're not going to find out what really happened until you talk to him."

I took a last sip of the water I'd been drinking. After last night I didn't want to touch another drink for a while.

"You know what, Yvonne?" I said after I set the glass down. "I had too much to drink last night. I've lost my appetite and I'm tired. So, I'm going to go lay down."

Her shoulders sank in defeat as she motioned for the waiter. "Can you please bring the check?" she asked. He nodded and she turned back to face me. "How long do you plan on being here?"

"I don't know. I could only book till tomorrow because they are holding some big conference and they're sold out Saturday. But I'm hoping someone doesn't show and I can just stay. Otherwise, I'll be moving to another hotel."

She looked around. Nineteenth-century art adorned the walls, and the distinctive decor showed why this had been deemed a historical landmark.

"Why didn't you go to the Four Seasons or something? This hotel looks like it's been here since the dinosaur age."

"It has. Since 1938, to be exact. I actually like the historic feel of this hotel. It's quaint."

She turned her nose up. "Whatever. You know what's better? Your house. You know that four-thousand-square-foot beauty Clark bought you?"

"Well, now he can sell it," I replied. "Or he and Dawn can move in together. Plenty of room for all her kids."

"Now you're being ridiculous," Yvonne said.

"You know what, I'm tired of talking about me," I said. "How are you? How's

Chad?" I said, referring to her fourteen-year-old son, who lived with her ex-husband.

"He's doing okay. Growing like a weed. He'll be here next weekend, over from San Antonio. I hate not having my son here, but I know boys need their fathers."

I nodded in sympathy. Yvonne had been embroiled in a bitter custody battle with her ex. Ultimately, she'd given in, knowing her teenaged son would fare better under her husband's guidance.

"What about your dad? Last time we talked, you said your sisters and brothers were talking about putting him in a home."

"Oh, they're doing more than talking about it now," she replied. "They're moving forward with their plan and I just can't believe it."

That momentarily caused my grief to shift onto someone else. "I'm so sorry to hear that," I said. "I can't imagine Mr. Ollie in a nursing home."

"*You* can't believe it? They might as well put him in the ground."

We talked about her family a little more, and when I felt her shifting the conversation back on me, I pulled out the bill that the waiter had slipped next to me as we talked, charged the dinner to my room, then stood. "Look, I appreciate everything. But I'm going to go lay down."

I could tell she didn't want to leave and I was prepared to just walk away, but she just said, "Okay. Fine." She stood with me. "But I will be checking on you tomorrow. And every day thereafter."

I managed a smile. Yvonne loved hard. "I wouldn't expect anything less. And Yvonne," I looked her straight in the eye, "please don't tell Clark where I am."

She turned her head, her gaze drifting around the bar area.

My voice got sterner. "Yvonne, you're my best friend. Not his," I reminded her.

She rolled her eyes and then leaned in to hug me. "Fine," she said. "But you better hurry up and figure this out. Because Clark is a good guy."

"Yeah. Good guys don't sleep with their late best friend's wife."

"Okay. He's a good guy who made a mistake."

"I'm sorry. What happened when you caught Darius cheating?" I asked. I had thought I was going to have to raise bail money when Yvonne caught her longtime boyfriend with another woman. She'd broken all the windows in his beloved Corvette, and he'd ending up calling the cops on her.

Luckily, I got her away before they arrived.

"I left him," Yvonne said, without blinking an eye, "because Darius was my boyfriend, not my husband. And he was evil and sadistic. Clark is not."

"Whatever," I said. "I love you. See you later and don't worry about me."

She hugged me and we said our goodbyes. I headed toward the elevator with the thought of divorce hanging over me like a threatening cloud.

This was not the way my life was supposed to be.

Sadness filled me as I realized, yet, this was the way it now was.

CHAPTER 5

Thoughts of divorce had consumed me all night. My parents had divorced. My grandparents had divorced. I had prayed that I would be able to break the cycle.

I was wrong.

Because there was no way a couple could survive this kind of betrayal.

Was there?

After meeting with Yvonne yesterday, I'd retreated to the bed and had let the sun set, then rise on my heartbreak. I pulled myself up against the headboard, the silence of the hotel room surrounding me, my best friend's words from yesterday lingering in my head.

Darius was evil and sadistic. Clark is not.

No, I could be as angry and hurt as I wanted, but my mind wouldn't even let me call Clark evil. What he did was evil, but the man that I'd met back when I was a sophomore in college and trying to stay out at the local hangout simply because I could, was anything but evil. The man who I had dated while he went to grad school and I began my career working as a reporter in Lawton, Oklahoma, was a God-fearing, devoted man. I fell in love with his caring heart. I watched him with those kids at the Boys & Girls Club and knew he was one of those special men that comes along once in a lifetime.

Boy, I couldn't have been more wrong. At the end of that perfectly painted picture, he was just a man. A cheating man.

As I sat in the bed, my mind replayed what had driven me to this hotel.

"Dawn, I need you to stop crying."

Normally, I wouldn't have paid my husband's voice any attention. Clark was always over at Dawn and Rob's house, so there was nothing unusual about seeing his car there when I first pulled up. But the hushed tone he had, and the fact that he was at Dawn's house when he was supposed to be at work, made my antenna rise.

I did as I usually did, walked around the side to come in on Dawn's back patio. For as long as I'd known Dawn and Rob, they never answered their front door — at least, for friends. We normally just came around to the back and tapped on the patio door, which led into their family room.

I had originally been on my way to meet my photographer to cover a story nearby when I decided to kill some time and detour to Dawn and Rob's. Clark had been friends with Rob since they played little league football together in southwest Houston. And after Rob's death, Clark had been a beacon of strength for Dawn and their four kids. So I wasn't thinking anything as I made my way down the side of the house, around the back, and toward the patio.

But the hushed tones halted my steps.

"I just feel so bad," Dawn said.

That made me inhale and then hold my breath as if I didn't want them to hear me breathing. I peered around the corner to see my husband holding Dawn in his arms. Again, normally, that wouldn't have bothered me.

But when he pulled away from her, he said, "We know that it will never happen again."

Those words ignited a sick flame in my stomach.

"It shouldn't have happened now," she said.

His voice cracked with pain. "I know. But it did. It's just that we can't look back. We have to look forward."

She moved away from him as my eyes

remained riveted. I was peering around the corner like a child spying on her parents.

"I just can't believe we did this to Savannah, to Rob. Oh, my God, what if Rob is looking down?" she cried as she buried her face in her hands.

"Dawn, we can't do this. We can't torture ourselves," Clark said. "We made a mistake, but we can't beat ourselves up about it. We have got to pull it together."

She looked up at him, her eyes red with tears. "What am I supposed to do the next time I see her?" Dawn gasped. "Am I supposed to just pretend that I didn't sleep with her husband?"

I held on to the wall to keep from toppling over. Then I did the only thing that was left to do. I stepped out and let my presence be known. Dawn spotted me first. And when Clark turned, their gasps were as one.

I stood, staring at both of them in disbelief.

"Oh, my God," Dawn said, horror blanketing her face. "Savannah, I'm so sorry."

I couldn't look at her.

The woman I thought was a friend.

The woman I confided in.

The woman I'd held up after her husband died.

No, I couldn't focus on Dawn Simmons right now. She hadn't made a vow before God to me. My husband had.

"Savannah . . ." That was the only word my husband could find.

"How could you do this?" I don't even know how I managed to find my voice.

"Babe, oh no. I . . . It's not . . . I'm so sorry. Let me explain," he stammered.

In the movies, when a woman catches her husband cheating then flees, I was that one who always talked about her not doing that. I was from Houston's Third Ward, where women didn't cower and run, where we administered beatdowns to side pieces. I had yelled at countless movie screens on what I'd do in that situation. But now that I was in that spot, the only thing I could think to do was turn and run.

Clark, of course, took off after me, calling my name as I bolted toward my car. But I must have channeled my high school track star years, because I was inside my Jaguar and peeling off by the time he made it to my car. And just like a scene out of a movie, he banged on my window as I backed out. I swear I wished there was a way that I could run him over. But I wasn't thinking clearly. And so I did the only thing that I could. I sped away as if my life depended on it.

Now here I was, in a hotel room, trying to

figure out my next move. Whatever that move was, I knew that it would involve finding the strength to move on from the man I had spent the last twelve years of my life married to.

I'd lost so much of my life to pity parties. I didn't know how I was going to pick up the pieces. I didn't know when. But I couldn't go back to that dark place I'd been in after the accident, and the only way I'd be able to do that would be to get out of this bed and find my strength.

I threw the covers back, got up, opened the blinds, and began the seemingly impossible task of getting my life together.

CHAPTER 6

Coffee. That's exactly what I needed to help with this never-ending hangover. So, after taking the elevator, I headed to the Starbucks in the lobby. I didn't bother looking at the menu and was about to order my usual Cafe Vanilla Mocha, but then I decided I needed a plain black coffee.

I had just given the barista my order when I heard, "When I said let's meet for coffee, I didn't know it would be this soon."

I turned around to see Wilson standing there with a smile on his face. I immediately wished I had made coffee in my room.

"Hi," I said.

"Good afternoon," he replied. "How are you today?"

The barista handed me my coffee and I thanked her and turned back to Wilson, my gaze shifting in shame. How did you look a man you'd almost had a one-night stand with in the eye?

"Better now," I said, holding up the coffee. When it was obvious he wasn't moving, I said, to say something, "So, I see you are still here."

"Actually, I'm about to head out. Since I couldn't get out the other night, I stayed an extra day to take care of some business. But the roads have cleared up and I need to get on back home. Gotta make up for missing my daughter's recital. I'm going to take her to dinner and to get her nails done."

"Sounds like fun. How old is she?"

"Twelve. My other two kids are grown. But my daughter lives with her mother, so I don't get to spend as much time as I would like with her."

We stepped out of the way to let the person behind us order, then stood in an uncomfortable silence for another moment before I said, "About the other night . . ."

He held up his hand. "Hey, I told you, no need for an explanation. I completely understand. Were you headed back to your room, or do you want to sit and talk over coffee?"

Because of what I had done, I really wanted to disappear. But something about Wilson's warm demeanor put me at ease. And since he was divorced, I wanted to talk to him about that process.

Wilson ordered his own cup of coffee, and

we took a seat at a table in the corner.

"So, let's address the elephant in the room," he began. "I completely understand about the other night. I don't think you're the type of woman who randomly takes men to her hotel room, or else the night would have ended differently." He flashed that Colgate smile. "But I do think you are going through some issues and it might help to talk about it."

"With a perfect stranger?" I said, giving a one-sided smile.

"Sometimes a stranger is perfect. Especially a stranger who has been through what you've been through."

I nodded, and before I knew it, I was saying, "So, you cheated on your wife?"

"Why do you automatically assume that it was me who did the cheating?" He chuckled.

My face filled with embarrassment. "Oh, I'm so sorry."

He smiled to put me at ease. "But you're right. It was me. The worst thing I ever did in my life. I loved her like crazy. And had my wife given me another chance, I would have spent the rest of my life making it up to her."

"Wow," I said, hesitating as I weighed my next words. "So, can you be honest? Why

54

would you cheat on your wife when you" —
I made air quotes — " 'loved her like
crazy'?"

He shrugged, not fazed by my sarcasm.
"Why do men cheat? Dumb. Not thinking.
It wasn't even a case of thinking the grass
was greener, because I knew it wasn't. I just
took a stupid risk. Of course, I could list all
the things my wife didn't do, but that list
would be short. In fact, my list of shortcom-
ings would probably be twice as long. My
wife didn't do anything to drive me away.
She kept the house. She worked. She didn't
nag. She didn't withhold sex. She was still
beautiful. She was everything I wanted."

I cocked my head and pursed my lips.
"And yet . . . still you cheated?"

He shrugged his right shoulder as he took
a sip of his coffee. "Cheating for some men
isn't as complicated as women think it is.
Lots of women make it about themselves.
And most of the time it has nothing to do
with the woman."

"That sounds like a cop-out," I told him.

"It may be, but it's the truth." He leaned
forward. The smell of his cologne tickled
my nose. Everything about this man was
sexy. Maybe I would use his number after
my divorce was final.

"But let me be clear," he continued. "I'm

not justifying cheating in any shape, form, or fashion. It's just the reality. Oftentimes, a man cheating on you is not a reflection on you. Sometimes we just do dumb stuff."

"What about when he cheats with someone you know?" I found myself saying.

"Whoa," he said, leaning back.

I nodded. "Exactly. She was his best friend's wife and a dear friend to the family."

"Wow. And his best friend hasn't put him in the hospital?" Wilson asked.

An image of Rob popped into my head. I couldn't even imagine how hurt he would be about this. "No. His best friend died a few months ago. Dawn — his wife — was supposedly heartbroken. I guess in the midst of their" — I made the air quotes again — " 'grief,' they found their way into each other's bed."

"Oh," he said. He took another sip, nodding like he was thinking. "Well, I know it's wrong and I know it hurts, but I wouldn't put a lot of stake in that. People always say men are physical and women are emotional. But I think a lot of people don't realize that men can be emotional as well. I think, based on what you just said, the two of them were just in an emotional place."

"So then they cry on each other's shoulder. They don't have sex," I snapped.

He raised his hands in innocence. "Hey. I can't defend the guy. All I can tell you is that I messed up the best thing that ever happened to me. And I regret it. I'll go to my grave regretting it. People do dumb things. They . . . *we* make bad decisions. Is it possible that he just made a horrible mistake and that 'once a cheater, always a cheater' philosophy is a bunch of bull?" He paused, giving his words time to sink in. "Has he done it before?" he asked when I didn't answer.

"No, not to my knowledge," I said. I don't know why, but I believed with all my heart that Clark wasn't a serial cheater.

"Do you think he'll do it again?" Wilson asked.

I was pensive for a moment, then said, "I mean, I'd like to say no, but I never thought he would do it in the first place."

Silence momentarily filled the air. Then, "Has he been trying to contact you?"

"Nonstop."

The sincerity on his face was touching. "My gut is on you don't have to worry about this again. You guys have been married how long?"

"Twelve years," I said.

"Have there been any unusual phone

calls? Any clandestine meetings or unexplained disappearances? Any indications at all that he's a serial cheater?"

"No," I replied without hesitation. Because there hadn't been. Or maybe I'd been too blind to see them.

"Serial cheaters usually leave some type of sign."

"Okay. So what if it was his first time? It doesn't excuse anything."

"I'm not saying it does. I'm just saying right now you're in an emotional place, and the last thing you need to do is make a decision based on that emotion."

I smiled. On top of being handsome and undeniably sexy, Wilson was a thoughtful and wise man. "You're just full of wisdom," I told him.

"I graduated magna cum laude from the School of Hard Knocks," he replied.

"Well, your next wife will be a very lucky woman," I said.

"I don't want a next wife. I want my last wife." He shrugged. "But it is what it is. The good thing is, she's forgiven me."

"Well, that's great," I said. "Maybe there's a chance you'll reunite."

He shook his head. "Nah, because she reminds me constantly that even forgiven sins have consequences. And this is the consequence. I have to watch her move on with someone else. While I was watering someone else's grass, someone else was watering mine."

I smiled. "That should be a blues song."

"It probably is."

"So, she wouldn't take you back because she'd found another man?" I asked.

He shook his head. "Of course, that's what I wanted to convince myself of. But I found some emails. Though he was there for her while I was doing my thing, she remained committed to me. Until she made the decision to finally leave. Even then she would only be friends with him until months after our divorce was finalized."

The way he talked about his ex-wife made my heart ache. There was no doubt that he still truly loved her.

"The bottom line is, she's found someone and is very happy. Are you ready for that?" he asked me.

I thought about it. I knew the answer to that was a resounding no. This hurt enough. Imagining Clark building a life with someone else tore at my insides.

"So I should stay with someone that hurt me just because I can't envision him moving on?"

"Absolutely not," Wilson replied. "You

should stay with him because you love him." Seeing his cup was empty, he stood. "I need to hit the road. Baby girl awaits. It's been a pleasure, Ms. Savannah." He took my hand and gently kissed it. "When I left you the other night, I hoped we would meet again, perhaps hook up and finish what we started. Right now, I just hope you work things out with your husband because I see it in your eyes. The love you have for him is real. Don't let something like that get away. One mistake does not define a man." He leaned down and kissed me on the cheek. "You take care of yourself."

He left me to simmer in his words.

Wilson had been gone almost an hour. My coffee was now lukewarm. And I was still sitting in the coffee shop thinking about his words.

I could throw around the d-word all I wanted, but Wilson was right — I loved my husband. But as my mind drifted back to my friendship with Dawn and Rob, I couldn't help but wonder if that love was enough to weather this storm.

My phone buzzed, snapping me out of my thoughts, and that's when I noticed the alert that my voice mail was full. I'd only brought the phone with me because my plan had been to call and check in with my job. I opened the visual voice mail and scanned the numbers. Most of the messages were from Clark, and I deleted them without listening. But I paused when I recognized one of the numbers as one of my sources'. I pressed the voice mail icon to listen.

"Hey, Savannah," the voice began. "This is Richard Carthage, give me a call ASAP. It's major."

The journalist in me pushed the heartbroken wife aside and quickly dialed his number.

CHAPTER 7

Richard Carthage had been a beacon of story ideas. And while the last thing I felt like doing was work, I punched in the number to call him back. He picked up the phone on the first ring.

"Savannah!"

"Hey, Richard, how's it going?" I asked.

"Got something big for you."

Despite the pain I was feeling, I was still a journalist to my core. So I immediately sat up and gave him my full attention.

"What's going on?" I asked.

"I'm at Texas Children's Hospital. A six-year-old bystander has been shot in what looks like a gang shooting in Stafford. A little girl. Her older sister was hit, too, and is in the hospital."

I frowned in confusion. That was tragic, but why in the world would Richard be calling me about a gang shooting?

"I know you're wondering what's the big

deal," he said as if he was reading my mind. "But this isn't an ordinary case. They were leaving a birthday party at the Main Event. The six-year-old was killed. Her eight-year-old sister is in critical condition." He paused, like he was about to deliver a cliffhanger. "The girl's mother is undocumented and INS has been notified. They're on their way to the hospital to pick her up to deport her."

"What?" I exclaimed. "Her daughter was just killed, another one is fighting for her life, and they're about to deport the mother? You've got to be kidding me."

"Nope. No one else knows about the story. It's yours if you want it. You'll have the exclusive scoop. Tomorrow, everyone will be all over this story."

"Oh, my God," I mumbled. I caught a glimpse of myself in the mirror. I looked a fiery mess. "I . . . I'm not at work today."

"Well, if you're busy, you can send someone else from your station. What about that Isiah guy?"

"You know how I've been busting my butt on this immigration beat. I'm not about to turn it over to another reporter. They already gave Isiah his own show over me. I'm not letting this slip away."

"Well, it's yours. I owe you from that last

story you did for me."

"I appreciate it, Richard." Could I really shake this funk I was in and go to work? While my boss had been understanding about my personal leave, she would completely understand why I would need to cancel that to cover this story. "Yeah, I'm on it," I decided.

"The mother doesn't know," Richard said. "But ICE will be here in about two hours."

"I'll be there."

That would give me time to go get some more clothes. I didn't have a choice. I didn't want to go home, and this was Pulitzer Prize–winning material. The last thing I needed was to be looking like an old hag as I broke the story.

I glanced at my reflection, trying to see how much I could clean up. My hair had lost all its curl and I hadn't brought any other work outfits or my curling iron to do my hair. No, I had to go home.

I contemplated calling the Boys & Girls Club to make sure Clark was at work. But everyone knew me there, so I didn't want to take the chance.

"Hey, Margie," I said, calling my boss once I was in my car and heading to my house.

"How are you?" she asked. "Feeling better?"

"I'm okay. But actually, I was calling because one of my contacts called me. Got a major story. Can you get a photog to meet me at Texas Children's in two hours?"

"What's going on?"

"Six-year-old girl was struck and killed by a stray bullet as she was leaving a birthday party at the Main Event in Stafford."

"Yeah, we got that call. I have a crew on it," Margie said.

"Well, the little girl's sister is in surgery and it's not looking good. And my source says a deportation order has just been executed for the mom."

"You have got to be kidding me!" Margie said. "They won't even let her grieve her daughter?"

"I know, right? Anyway, it's an exclusive."

I knew any days I had missed had been forgiven because if there was anything to send my boss into utopia, it was an exclusive story.

"I'll have a photog there in two hours."

I thanked her and told her I'd have the story for the news tonight.

Now I just needed to put aside my personal life and focus on my job.

When I pulled onto my street, I saw that Clark's car wasn't parked in the driveway. I was grateful for small blessings as I dashed into the house to change.

I tried to do something with my hair, but I couldn't contain my frizz and didn't have time to flat-iron it, so I just moussed my hair down and pulled it back into a bun.

I was putting on makeup when I heard the chime of the door opening. I silently cursed myself for not putting my makeup on in the car.

"Savannah!" Clark yelled. His footsteps pounded up the stairs. "You came back!" he said, stopping in the doorway to our bedroom.

I glared at my husband. The man I'd thought was my forever love.

"I came back to get some more clothes." I stepped around him.

"No, wait, baby. We have to talk." He reached for me, and I immediately stepped out of his grasp.

"There is nothing for us to talk about," I said.

"Please. You have to hear me out."

I stopped and glared at him. "I don't have

66

to do anything but wait for you to get out of my way."

He held his hands up in defense, but said, "Savannah, please?"

"Clark, I don't have time to do this with you. I have somewhere to be."

He moved to block me again. His face was frantic. My husband was usually calm and cool, so I knew he had to be scared crazy. "I'm not letting you go until you hear me out."

"What are you going to do, hold me against my will?"

"I just need to explain."

I exhaled my exasperation. "There is nothing to explain. I have an exclusive story I'm working on, and I do not have time to do this with you."

"Okay, but just hear —"

"No!" I pushed past him. "Go tell it to Dawn."

"Savannah, please." He began following me down the stairs. In his state, I had no doubt Clark would follow me to the hospital for my news story, and I definitely didn't need that. So I turned to him, and he stopped on the bottom step. "Look," I said, "let me go do this and I'll come back and hear you out. Is that fine?"

He shifted like he wanted to protest, but

the look on my face must have told him not to push me, because he simply said, "Fine. You'll come back by the house? How long will you be at your story?"

I rolled my eyes but said, "Yes. I'll come back in a few hours, after I go live for the six o'clock news."

That sent a wave of relief over him and he nodded. "Okay, I'll be here."

I turned to leave without saying another word.

"I love you," he called out after me.

I let the door slam on his words. And my lie. Because I had no intention of coming back anytime soon.

CHAPTER 8

As a journalist, I'd seen my share of heart-breaking stories. But nothing had torn at me like the story I'd just filed. I don't know if it was because I was in an emotional place, but when they ripped Lupe Garcia from that hospital waiting room, I cried.

Her wail would stay with me. The cold, heartless ICE agents, who dragged her away as she begged to stay and wait for her daughter coming out of surgery, would haunt me forever. The doctors had pleaded. Even I pleaded, but they would not be moved. It was the evilest thing I'd ever witnessed. Apparently, Ms. Garcia had already been deported once, nine years ago, so the ICE agents showed no sympathy.

Her child had been killed, another injured, and they wouldn't even let the poor woman grieve. Normally, I kept my opinion out of my news stories, but when I went live on the six o'clock news, I didn't bother with objectivity. I let my disdain be shown.

So when I was leaving the hospital and my live shot, and saw my boss's name on my cell phone, I knew she was about to chew me out.

"Hey, Margie," I said, bracing myself for my verbal chastising.

"Savannah!" she sang. "That was frigging awesome! I know all the other stations are scrambling."

Her enthusiasm over our exclusivity apparently took precedence over any anger about me interjecting my opinion.

"Good. Glad you're pleased," I replied.

"Oh, I'm more than pleased," she said. "Hate to ask but can you come back and go live for the ten?"

I had known that request was coming, so I was already prepared. "Sure, I have to go take care of some things. I'll get an update, see if I can get a statement from INS, and be ready to go at ten."

"Awesome. That's why you're my superstar," she said. "I'll check in with you later."

Her excitement made me feel good. I took my job seriously and loved working for Margie. Besides, over the past few hours I hadn't thought about Clark or my situation. So obviously work was good for me.

But as I navigated down I-10 back toward

the Markham, I knew going back to the hotel would give me time to rekindle my pity party. So I made the decision to swing by Starbucks and try and make some calls and dig up some more information, to get a different spin on my story tonight. The only issue was this rush-hour traffic.

I inhaled, decided not to let rush hour get me worked up, then turned up the radio to relax while I took my time navigating through the traffic.

I smiled when the Temptations began singing about sunshine on a cloudy day. The song immediately took me back . . .

"I've got sunshine on a cloudy day." Rob's voice resonated throughout the karaoke club. The crowd was eating it up. "When it's cold outside, I've got the month of May."

"Don't quit your day job," my husband yelled from our table in the back of the room.

"Leave my baby alone," Dawn said. She cupped her hands around her mouth and shouted, "Go on, baby. Sing for mama."

Our table erupted in laughter as Rob belted out the entire three verses of the Temptations' song. It was good to get out after months of locking myself in the house. I'd taken a medical leave of absence from work and restricted myself to the house. I'd come out of my grief, but every time I had fun, I felt guilty, so it was rare for me to indulge. Though, tonight, I'd finally taken Clark up on his offer and headed out for a night on the town with Rob and Dawn, his wife of sixteen years. The four of us had been inseparable before my accident. I knew Rob had been Clark's rock through my whole ordeal. And I genuinely loved him, not just for that but because he was the kind of friend that every wife wanted her husband to have. By default, Dawn and I had become really good friends as well.

A chorus of catcalls for "More!" and pats on the back surrounded Rob as he made his way back over to us. His dimpled smile and hazel eyes lit up the table.

"So, do you think Atlantic Records is gonna sign me?" he said as he slid into his seat.

"No, you're going to have us signing. You see, we're going to need sign language since we're all deaf after that number," Clark said, patting his ear like something was stuck in it.

"Ignore him, baby," Dawn said, leaning over to kiss her husband. "He's just mad because he doesn't have chops like you."

"I know, honey. I'm used to the jealousy by now," Rob said, brushing imaginary lint off his shoulder. "I just brush the haters off."

We all laughed as someone else went to the mic.

"Come on, Clark. Your turn. You've got next, right?" Rob said.

Clark leaned back in his seat, picked up his glass, and took a sip of the brown liquor. "I wish I would."

"Yeah, I would like to see that," I said. No way was my husband about to get up in front of a room and make a fool of himself.

Clark endured some more teasing before we all turned our attention to the petite woman belting out Whitney Houston's "I Will Always Love You."

"Excuse me," Clark said, flagging down a waitress, "can we get another round for me and the ladies and a seltzer for my boy here?" He pointed at Rob. "Make sure you put a little lemon drop or some Fruity Pebbles or something in his drink."

"Whatever," Rob said, unfazed by the usual roasting he got because he didn't drink, not even socially. "You can knock me all you want, but when your liver is all torn up, don't ask me to change your diaper."

We all laughed as Dawn grabbed my arm.

"Okay, come on, our turn," Dawn told me as the Whitney singer wrapped up.

"Our turn for what?" I asked.

"We're going to do En Vogue 'Don't Go' or

The Supremes 'Stop! in the Name of Love,' "
Dawn said.

I snatched my arm away. "You can do whatever you want. I'm not getting up there." I leaned back like Clark had done just moments ago.

"Come on, Savannah," Dawn pleaded.

"Do it. Do it. Do it," Clark and Rob said in unison as they pounded on the table.

"You have a lot of nerve," I told my husband. He flashed a wicked grin at me.

"Come on, girl. Let's show these men how it is done," Dawn said.

"You know what? You're right," I said, standing up and following my friend to the stage.

We performed "Stop! in the Name of Love" and, like Rob, had the crowd going wild.

By night's end, I was tipsy and tired. As we bid our friends farewell, I couldn't wait to get home with my husband.

We had actually been home an hour when my phone rang. I had just dozed off, but I picked it up, hit the talk button, and immediately heard Dawn screaming.

"Savannah, where's Clark?"

I yawned. "He's lying next to me, asleep. Why?"

"I was trying to call him," she cried.

I sat up in the bed once I realized the panic in her voice. "You know he turns his phone off. I need you to calm down and tell me what's going on."

"It's . . . It's Rob. H-he went . . . I left my credit card at the k-karaoke bar . . . and the bar . . . back . . . He went back . . . he w-went back to get it." She was sobbing so hard her sentence was barely coherent. "And on the way back . . . the police . . . they said . . . they said . . ."

"Okay, sweetie. Calm down. Where are you?"

"We're at Sugar Land Methodist," she cried.

My heart tightened. "The hospital? Is Rob all right?" I leaned over and shook Clark.

"I-I don't know."

"All right." I jumped up. "We're on our way."

"Please hurry," she said.

Clark was staring at me as I hung up the phone. "What's going on? Who was that?" he asked, his voice groggy like he'd been in a deep slumber already.

"It's Dawn," I said. "There's been an accident." I took a deep breath before I pushed out my next words. "It's Rob."

"What?" he said, all traces of sleep gone. "Is he all right?"

"I don't know anything. I'm assuming he is since he's at the hospital. Dawn just . . ." I couldn't finish my sentence as Clark jumped up out of the bed. I grabbed a T-shirt and leggings out of a drawer and quickly put them on. Within minutes, we were in the car.

Neither of us said a word as we sped down Highway 6 from our Pearland home.

"Babe, slow down," I finally said after the second time someone honked at us for cutting them off. I had never seen my husband so panicked.

I was grateful when we finally arrived to the hospital, because I had been sure Clark was going to kill us on the way here. When we arrived at the waiting room, Dawn was in tears. As soon as we walked in, she raced over and threw her arms around Clark's neck.

"Oh, my God. It's not good, it's not good," she cried.

"It's okay," he said, squeezing her, before pulling back and looking her in the eyes. "Tell me what happened."

She fought back her sobs as she said, "It's just not fair . . . He doesn't drink but . . . a drunk driver hit him."

I was frozen.

"But . . . he's going to be okay, right?" Clark said.

"I don't know. The ER doctor said . . ." She stopped talking as a doctor appeared in the waiting room doorway.

The way he stood at the edge of the doorway, like he didn't want to approach us, sent my heart in a tailspin. He moved closer to Dawn, who was hanging on to Clark like he was her lifeline.

"Mrs. Simmons?" the doctor said.

Dawn nodded.

The doctor shifted as if, even though he'd done this countless times, it was one of the most dreaded things he had to do. "I'm sorry to tell you this . . ."

"Noooo . . ." Dawn wailed as her knees gave out. I raced to keep her from falling to the floor, because Clark was in shock as well.

"You're sorry for what?" Clark said, each word punctuated with pain. "That he's having a hard time? That he's injured? What are you sorry about?"

The doctor exhaled loudly. "Mr. Simmons didn't make it."

Dawn's wails mixed with my husband's and filled the entire waiting room.

We'd had to stay with Dawn for the next forty-eight hours. She'd spent most of that time sedated. We were there as she told the kids. And we'd been by her side nearly every day since that happened. Only somewhere along the line, my husband's comfort had found its way into her bed. And for that, I would never forgive either one of them.

The Lord heals the brokenhearted and binds

up their wounds.

Ugh. I don't know why that verse popped into my head. There was no healing from this wound. But as I approached the Highway 6 exit — the exit to Dawn's house — I knew I couldn't even start to heal until I faced the snake that bit me. And that thought made me veer right and off the freeway.

The look on Dawn's face told me I was the last person she'd ever expected to see.

"Oh, my God, Savannah," she said, tears springing to her eyes. "I was hoping I could talk to you."

I glared at her, trying to figure out if I should snatch her by her eighteen-inch Malaysian Yaki, or just hear her out. I decided on the latter.

"Yeah, we need to talk," I said.

She stepped aside and motioned for me to step inside. "Please come in."

"Nah, I won't be long," I announced.

I'd never seen Dawn so nervous. But I'm sure she wondered if I'd snap, because my tone was so calm. She pulled the belt on her robe tighter. It was seven o'clock in the evening. Why was she already in her robe?

"I never meant —" she began.

"How long have you been screwing my

78

husband?" I said, cutting her off.

"It was just the one time," she said, stepping out onto the porch and closing her front door. I guess she didn't want her children to hear what a whore she was. "Savannah, I'm so sorry. You have every right to be angry."

I rolled my eyes and suppressed my curse words so I didn't give her the satisfaction of losing it.

"What Clark and I did was a onetime occurrence," she continued. "We're both so sick about it. We didn't mean for it to happen."

My bravado gave way to my pain. "Your kids call me auntie" was all I could say. "I thought we were friends."

"I know," she replied, the trickling tears now flowing full stream. "I don't expect you to understand. I don't even understand. I don't even like Clark like that. I mean, I have never even looked at him that way."

"So, you make it a habit to sleep with guys you don't like like that?" I snapped.

"No, I mean . . . I love Clark . . . but it's not sexual."

I cocked my head at her.

She seemed to be getting flustered. "I mean, what I'm trying to say is it was a mistake, a horrible, horrible mistake. I just missed Rob so much and Clark . . . he just . . . everything about him reminded me of Rob."

"Well, you can have him," I said, tired of hearing this sob story. "So he can replace Rob and be a daddy to your kids. He'll get the kids he wants, and you'll get your replacement husband."

"The only child he wants is the one you guys were going to adopt."

A pain shot through my heart. I wanted to summon my Third Ward roots and slap her for mentioning the child that we'd dreamed of.

"There's a child out there that needs you."

"No, a child needs a committed couple. Clark isn't committed to me."

"Yes, he is. He loves you so much."

"I would hate to see how he'd treat me if he didn't."

She bit down on her lip, wiped away the tears from her cheeks. "All I'm saying is please forgive him. I don't expect you to ever forgive me."

"Good," I said. "I'm glad we got that out of the way."

She grimaced, but I really didn't care. The fact that she was really trying to convince me to stay in a marriage she'd destroyed disgusted me.

"Just don't walk away from Clark," she said.

Her saying my husband's name infuriated me. "You know what? This was a mistake. I don't know what I thought I would accomplish by coming here. You and Clark can go to hell." I turned to walk away.

"The kids and I are moving. Away," she said just as I stepped off the porch.

That made me stop again. My first thought as I turned back to face her was *Good riddance.* But I thought about her children and the relationship I'd developed with all of them. Another ache shot through my body. I didn't say a word, though, as she continued talking.

"It's been so hard here without Rob." She ran her hands up and down her thighs like she was nervous. "And it's difficult raising the kids alone. So I'm going back to Alabama, to be near my mom."

"How does Trinity feel about all of that?" I said, knowing her oldest loved her school. She was a cheerleader and senior class vice president. I could only imagine how she would take the news.

"I haven't told her yet. She's going to be devastated, but she'll survive."

This transgression not only ruined my life. It was ruining the lives of those innocent children. "So are you running from my husband?" I couldn't help but ask.

"This has nothing to do with Clark. It's the void. The hole in my heart I feel about losing Rob. Everything here reminds me of him." She lowered her head again. "Clark reminded me of him. That's all it was." She swallowed, managed to look me in the eyes again. "I'm hoping that the move will give the children and me a fresh start."

She wasn't going to get to me. Even though she was using her children to try.

"Well, have a nice life," I said. I turned again to leave, and this time she reached out to stop me. My eyes immediately went down to her hand on my arm, which she quickly moved away.

"I'm just telling you that we're leaving, so you don't have to worry about me. It would never happen again, regardless of whether I stayed or not. But I'll be gone, so you won't have to be reminded of our horrible indiscretion. Give Clark another chance. Just forgive him. Begin the healing process."

"I don't take advice from whores," I said.

That seemed like it stung, but again, I didn't care. I didn't care about the pain written all over her face. It would never match the pain that was written all over my heart.

"I will spend the rest of my life regretting this. I hope one day you can find it in your heart to forgive us," she said. "My children — and I — are going to miss you."

A dejected aura hung over her. She looked like she wanted to hug me, but I guess she knew better, because she simply turned and walked back into the house. I pushed away any feelings about her children's departure as I made my way to my car. As I climbed in the driver's seat, I pushed down the bile building in my throat.

How in the world could I ever recover from this pain?

CHAPTER 9

I had a dream last night. In it, Clark and I had two children — the one I lost and the one we were adopting. The dream had been so vivid. We were all enjoying Thanksgiving dinner. Even my mother was there, along with extended family members. Everyone at the table was so happy and my children wouldn't stop smiling.

I'd awakened from that dream in tears. That was a life I would never know.

I swung my legs over the side of the bed and sat up. After my live shot last night, I'd come back to the hotel and turned off my phone because Clark had started calling around seven and hadn't stopped. Seeing Dawn had only exacerbated my pain, so I had come back to the room and cried myself to sleep.

Now I needed to pull myself together. Lift this emotional cloud that hung over me. Maybe a shower would help me feel better.

But as I stepped into the bathroom, I realized I had no towels and my room hadn't been cleaned in the four days that I'd been here. I had the Do Not Disturb sign on my door. Since I had told the front desk that I would call when I was ready for the room to be cleaned, I couldn't be mad that I didn't have fresh towels.

I opened the door, hoping to see housekeeping in the hallway so that I could get some towels. I spotted the housekeeper's cart at the end of the hall, so I put up the door bolt to keep my door from locking and walked down the hall.

The door to Room 320 was open, and I assumed the housekeeper was in there cleaning. I was about to tap on the open door when I heard her on the phone.

"Imelda, you've got to stop crying," the woman said. "Hector is not the first man who cheated and he won't be the last one. I told you, you can get past this."

Of course, I didn't mean to eavesdrop, but I had to stop. *Was everyone in the world cheating?* I was riveted to her conversation. The housekeeper was so passionate yet soothing in her words.

"All I'm saying," she said, her voice rich with a thick Latin-American accent, "is you just have to pray. If he's willing to do the work, then you can make this work."

If he's willing to do the work, then you can make this work.

I knew Clark would do whatever necessary, put in as much work as needed. But I didn't see how that would ever be enough.

I felt some kind of way about listening to her conversation. So I gently tapped the door.

"Excuse me," I said. "Sorry to interrupt."

She stopped making the bed and looked up at me, startled.

"I'll have to call you back," she said, turning off her phone and dropping it into her apron. "I'm s-so sorry," she stammered. "It was an emergency."

"Hey. It's okay," I said. "I'm not going to report you."

She seemed to relax. "We're not supposed to be on our phones."

I gave her a reassuring smile. "It sounds like you were a big help to whomever you were talking to."

She shrugged, like she dispensed helpful advice every day. "My friend is having a hard time," she said. Concern filled her eyes, but then it shifted from her friend to me.

"Are you okay?" she asked.

My hand instinctively went to my hair,

and I turned and saw my reflection in the mirror. I saw why she asked. My eyes were puffy and the makeup from my live shot was smeared since I hadn't bothered to wash my face before bed. My bun had unraveled and my hair was also matted; I looked like I'd been on someone's battlefield.

"I'm okay," I lied. "I'm sorry to disturb you. I just wanted to get some fresh towels."

She scurried over to her cart and handed me two towels. "Are you in 316?" she asked.

I nodded.

"Okay. I've been told not to disturb you. But are you sure you don't want me to clean your room?"

I thought about it. I probably did need the sheets changed and some tidying up, but I didn't feel like leaving. "If you don't mind straightening up around me," I said.

"Of course," she replied. "I'm just finishing up here. I can come right after. It will only take me a few minutes."

I smiled in appreciation and made my way back down to my room. I'd wait until she finished to jump in the shower. In the meantime, I took a seat at the desk and pulled out my laptop to draft an email to my boss. After my exclusive report, I was in her good graces. But barring any more breaking news, I knew that I needed at least a week off. Since I never called in sick and rarely took vacation, I had plenty of days. Because I didn't want to get Margie in any trouble with the higher-ups, I wanted to put my leave request in writing. I knew I was going to have to make a decision soon because I couldn't stay holed up in this hotel forever, but I needed a few more days.

"Housekeeping," the housekeeper called as she tapped on my door.

"Come on in."

She flashed a warm smile. "I won't take long."

"It's okay," I said. "I'm just going to sit here at the desk and do some work if that's all right."

"Of course." She immediately began changing the sheets. When I opened up my Gmail account, I saw four new emails from Clark. I clicked on the first one.

Please come home. I'm so sorry.

I sent the message to the trash. Then I dumped the other three without bothering to open them. I don't know what made me say anything, but I turned to the housekeeper and said, "I wasn't trying to eavesdrop, but your friend, her husband cheated on her?"

The woman turned to me, a sad expression across her face. "Yes, Hector is a good man, though. He just made a really bad mistake."

"That seems to be going around," I mumbled. "What's your name?"

"Anna. Anna Rodríguez."

"Have you been working here awhile?"

I don't know why I was making small talk. I think it was just a habit of mine as a reporter. The best stories seemed to come organically.

But Anna didn't seem to mind. It almost felt like she was appreciative that a guest thought enough of her to hold a conversation.

"Six years." She smiled. "Blessed to have a job." She patted the bedspread down, then fluffed the pillow.

"Well, I'll be in and out." She paused as she was about to walk past me. "And I don't mean to offend you, but whatever it is that is burdening your soul, know that it will work out. With God, all things are possible."

I smiled. "Yeah. For some of us anyway."

She didn't flinch. "For all of us. Always. It may not be the way we want it to work out. Or even when. We may not understand it. But He'll work it out in our best interest."

That conversation made me uneasy. At

some point I'd have to reconcile my feelings of abandonment by God, but now, during this painful process, wasn't the time.

I noticed the gold chain on her neck. "Are those your children?" I said, noting the names written in cursive and connected by hearts.

She fingered the necklace and her face lit up. "Yes, they are my world. I have four children. My three youngest are my pride and joy," she said. "My oldest, love him something crazy. But he . . . he is a challenge. He's a good kid who has taken up with the wrong crowd, so I'm staying in prayer."

It was obvious this woman sought her solace in God, but that just no longer worked for me. After my accident, when I prayed, I came up empty. When my prayers of motherhood weren't answered, I just got to a point where I stopped praying.

"Oh, yeah," I said, the thought of prayer reminding me of the tattered book. But when I stood, I knocked my purse over and several items toppled out.

"Here, let me help," Anna said, kneeling to pick up my things. "I knew you looked familiar," she said as she gathered my business cards. "You're the lady reporter from

Channel 26," she said, smiling in recognition.

I nodded. "That's me, but please excuse my appearance."

"I watch you every night. You're even prettier in person."

My hand instinctively went to my hair. How anyone could call me pretty right now was beyond me. "Thank you," I replied anyway.

"Can I have a card?"

"Absolutely," I said.

Anna dropped the card in her apron pocket, then resumed cleaning the room.

"That is what I was going to ask about." I picked up the Bible off the nightstand. "This was in this room. Does it belong here or did the last guest forget it?"

Anna looked at the book, then shrugged. "I've never seen it before. Not sure if it belongs here. Do you want me to take it to Lost and Found?"

I thought about it. "Nah, I'll just leave it here. Maybe someone can use it." I dropped it back on the nightstand. "Thank you. And Anna, it was nice to meet you."

"Nice to meet you as well." She paused as she headed toward the door. "Remember, sometimes it may feel like we're walking this journey alone. But those are the times that

He's carrying you. You're here in this room for a reason. God wants you to be still so you can hear what He wants for your life."

She smiled and left the room.

Be still.

Hmph. I'd been still and I still didn't know what I was going to do.

CHAPTER 10

There's no loyalty among friends.

That's all I could think as I peered out the peephole of my hotel room.

My husband was standing on the other side, looking like he hadn't slept in days. He had bags under his eyes, his pupils were pierced with redness. And he was here, outside Room 316. The only way he'd have known I was here was if Yvonne had opened her big mouth.

"I see you looking at me," Clark said. "Open the door, Savannah, please? You said we could talk."

"I lied. Just like you did when you claimed to love me."

"I haven't lied to you, Savannah. I do love you. With all my heart," he pleaded.

"What do you want?" I shouted. "How did you convince Yvonne to sell me out?"

"She knows how much I love you," he replied.

I was going to kill Yvonne. I sighed, then said, "Clark, go away. I don't want to talk to you."

He stared like he was trying to see through the door. "So, are you just going to stay holed up in this hotel forever?"

"I'm going to stay here until I'm ready to leave," I yelled.

"Then I'm going to stay here until you're ready to talk to me."

I peeked out of the peephole again. "You're going to be waiting a mighty long time."

"Cool," he said, taking off his jacket and setting it on the floor. I was surprised that he wasn't at work. He was the director of the Boys & Girls Club of Houston, and I knew they had a big event today. The fact that he was here and not there spoke volumes.

I peered down until I couldn't see him. "I'm going to call Security," I yelled.

"And I'm going to make a scene, and you know you don't like scenes," he replied.

I waited a few moments as I gathered my thoughts. I liked it here. The last thing I wanted was to get kicked out. Finally, I leaned back in toward the door and said, "So, you're just going to bully me into talking with you?"

"That's what marriage is, Savannah. You don't run from your problems. You stand strong and face them head-on," he announced.

"Don't preach to me about what marriage is," I yelled back through the door. I inhaled, trying to calm myself down. "Just go away, Clark."

"Nope," he replied. "I'll stay right here until you hear me out."

Clark could be so headstrong. He was strong, period. As I stood by the door, my mind raced back to the only time I'd seen him falter.

My husband was living under a cloud of grief. I understood because it had been my home for months. But still, I tried to do what I could to bring him out.

"Clark, maybe you should go talk to someone," I told him one day after he'd been sitting on the patio smoking a cigar for three hours.

"Not now, Savannah," he replied, not even looking my way. "I just want to be left alone."

Instead of doing what I'd been doing since Rob's death — closing the door and going back into the house — I walked outside and sat next to him on the patio sofa.

"I miss Rob, too," I said.

95

Clark was silent.

"But it's like you told me, at some point you have to move on."

With a slow turn, he looked at me and frowned. "Really, Savannah? It's been a month, and your answer is to just move on? You think you can just say get over it and all is well?" he snapped. "You, of all people, know it's not that easy."

"No, you know that's not what I'm saying." I was trying to recall all the things he had said to me to pull me out of my grief, but over the past month it seemed as if everything I'd said had been the wrong thing, so I remained hesitant to push him.

"I was just thinking —"

"Can you give me some time, please?" he asked, cutting me off.

I let out a heavy sigh. I knew his irritation wasn't with me, but with his struggle to deal with Rob's death. I just hated that he was shutting me out of the healing process.

The sound of Clark singing "At Last" brought me out of the past. My stomach fluttered against my will. That was the song that had been playing when he proposed. And we had our first dance to the song at our wedding. It was our song.

I shook away the thought.

No! I screamed inside, trying desperately to push away the memory. Clark and I no longer had a song. And he could be stubborn, but so could I. He could sit out there all night for all I cared.

Chapter 11

Anderson Cooper had gone off. Two episodes of *Family Feud* had played. And *Will & Grace* had graced my screen for an hour.

And still Clark waited.

I'd peeked through the peephole several times over the last few hours. I'd stopped talking to him and refused to answer his questions, thinking in time he'd just go away.

He hadn't.

Clark was plopped on the floor, his back against the door. He almost fell back when I cracked the door open.

"Are you really going to sit out here in the hallway all night?" I said. "It's one in the morning."

He jumped up and put his foot in the door like he was scared I'd slam it back shut. He didn't know I would still slam it, even with his foot in it.

"Savannah, please, baby, just hear me out.

98

Let me talk to you."

I inhaled, then figured the sooner we could hash this out, the sooner I could begin the paperwork for my divorce. I didn't say a word as I stepped aside to let him in.

"Sweetheart, let me explain," he immediately began after he stepped inside.

"So, you can explain sleeping with our friend? Your best friend's wife?" I let the door close, but didn't move into the room. I didn't want him to get comfortable.

Shame filled his face. "There's no justification," he said. "I was wrong. Dead wrong."

I waited for him to make up an excuse, to add a "but." Instead he stood there in silence.

"Yeah, you were dead wrong." I folded my arms. "So, how long have you two been having an affair? How long have you been smiling in my face, probably laughing behind my back while you did it? Were you sleeping together when Rob was alive?"

I knew better than that because when I came up on them, I'd heard the pain in both of their voices. And Dawn claimed it was a onetime occurrence. Besides, if Clark was capable of more than that, then I truly did not know him at all. I knew that they hadn't been sneaking around for years, but this was the picture I wanted to paint right now.

"I would never betray Rob like that," he said.

"But you'd betray me?"

He winced like he regretted his choice of words, but I wasn't letting up. "And it's okay to betray him when he's gone?"

"Neither Dawn nor I expected or wanted this to happen," Clark said.

"Expected or wanted what? Me to find out?"

"No, it's not that at all."

"So, her husband dies and she just decides she'll steal mine?" I snapped before he could wade into his explanation.

"No." He walked into the room, as if putting some distance between us would make this easier. "We both . . . It's just the void with Rob. We got lost in our grief."

"I lost Rob, too," I screamed, then lowered my voice before someone called Security. "I don't know how many times I have said that over the past six months."

"I know that but . . ." He began pacing back and forth across the room. "Rob was like a brother to me."

"Oh, that makes it worse. That means you had no problem sleeping with your 'brother's' wife?" I said.

He stopped, looked at me, and with conviction said, "I'm not going to try and justify it. Why it happened," he said. "It should not have happened."

I stepped closer to him. I wanted him to see my pain up close and personal. I wanted him to feel it, dance with it. I didn't want him to be able to run from it. "Where did it happen? Did you screw her in our bed?"

"Come on, now. You know I would never do anything like that," he said.

I edged away from him, unable to stomach his presence.

"I don't know anything," I said. "I thought I knew my husband enough to know that he wouldn't sleep with his best friend's wife. But obviously, I was wrong."

"You have every right to be mad at me," he said.

"Oh, thank you for giving me permission," I replied. I walked over to the window and stared out, keeping my back to him while I tried to stop the flow of tears.

"All I'm asking is for you to go deep in your heart and look for forgiveness. I can't lose you," he said.

That caused me to spin like I was starring in *The Exorcist.* I no longer cared about the tears. "You don't want to lose me?" I asked, incredulous. "You should have thought about that before you slept with her. I mean,

I was coming over there to bring her child tickets to a concert. A child that I looked at as my own niece."

"And they're still family."

"Like hell," I said, pushing by him again. I sat on the bed, but when an image of Wilson flashed through my mind, I jumped up.

"Savannah, what happened was a huge mistake," Clark continued. "I don't love her. She doesn't love me. Not like that anyway. Grief brought us together."

"Oh, that's such a convenient excuse," I said.

"You know firsthand what grief can do to a person."

I glared at him, stunned that he would go there. "Oh, so because I was in the depths of despair, I should understand, right? I should understand why you landed in Dawn's bed. When I was grieving, I kept to myself. I didn't find solace in the arms of another man."

"I know," he said, his face cloaked in desperation. "I know how you dealt with your grief because I was right there helping you through it. You shut me out and I was still there."

"You shut me out in grieving Rob. But I guess that's because you preferred to commiserate with Dawn."

102

"I know. I know. I shut down. But it's like Dawn got it. Dawn felt as close to him as I did. My sense of loss matched hers."

I knew that Rob and Clark had had an unbreakable bond. I knew that he was heartbroken over his death. But it wasn't my fault that he wouldn't let me in to help him heal.

"Oh, I'm so happy that you and Dawn have something in common," I said. Then, deciding to stop fighting the tears, I just let them flow. "I didn't betray you. I would've never betrayed you," I said, my voice cracking.

Clark tried to take my hand. "Savannah, if you give me a chance, I will spend the rest of my life making it up to you. We can go to counseling. We can do whatever you like."

The sarcasm left me. In its place was only pain. "I can't do it, Clark," I whispered. "How can I ever heal from this betrayal?"

"We have healed from worse," he said, squeezing my hands tighter. I was willing myself to snatch my hands away. But my body betrayed me. "Much worse," he added.

And with those words, I knew he was right. But I didn't see how in the world I could ever come back from this.

"Just come home. I'll stay in another room until you're ready. But we can't work on us if you're not at home."

I shook my head. "Not yet, Clark."

Relief passed over him. "Okay, at least you didn't say never."

I finally pulled away, headed back to my safe space at the window.

"Take however long you need, but not too long," he continued.

When I turned and cut my eyes at him, he quickly added, "Please?" Clark didn't wait for my reply as he reached in his jacket pocket and pulled out an oversized manila envelope.

"When you get time, there are some things in here I want you to look through. I want you to know how much I love you. Everything in this envelope will help you understand just how much. I love you, Savannah Graham."

He leaned in and kissed my forehead, and this time I didn't resist. But I didn't relax until he was gone.

CHAPTER 12

Clark had been gone for two hours. But his words were still right there with me.

My heart was screaming for me to go home, but my head was trying to be the voice of reason. My heart wanted me to forgive; my head wanted to wallow in my anger. But I was tired of being angry.

I gently ran my finger along the manila envelope that Clark had left. It was probably some long note about why I should give him a second chance. He'd won my heart by writing me love letters when we first started dating after I'd moved from Lawton and began reporting in Oklahoma City and he was working his way up the ranks of the Boys & Girls Club in Dallas. His letters had touched my soul, and for that reason I almost threw this new envelope in the trash. But I could feel that there were several items inside, and curiosity got the best of me.

I sat on the edge of the bed, flipped the

envelope over, gently eased it open, and dumped the contents out on the bed.

The first thing that caught my eye was our wedding picture. I picked it up and didn't know whether to smile or cry. This had been the happiest day of my life, followed only by the day I found out I was pregnant. But this was back when I believed in fairy tales and happily ever after. Back when I didn't know that my dream would end with a nightmare.

I tossed the picture aside and picked up a card. The cursive writing on the front let me know it was one of those Mayflower sappy greeting cards. I opened the card, read the heartwarming message about a "forever love," then Clark's handwritten note at the bottom.

While you grieve, I'm here.

When you're finished grieving, I'll still be here. I'm never going anywhere.

Love you always and forever, Clark

That brought a tear to my eye. Clark had slid this card to me one of the days when I wouldn't get up off the sofa.

I sifted through some more items from the bag until I came to one of those plastic stretchy bracelets. I picked it up and read the inscription: *The Lord heals the broken-*

hearted and binds up their wounds.

Clark had slid this onto my wrist one night as I slept. I'd worn it the entire time I was trying to recover from my grief. I'd tossed it once God refused to honor my wish to get pregnant again. I couldn't believe Clark had dug the bracelet out of the trash and hung on to it all this time.

I fell back against the headboard. I didn't want these things to get to me, yet they were. I hated that all of this was affecting me. All of this was reminding me that, while I despised what Clark had done, it didn't change the fact that I loved him from the bottom of my heart.

After years of not praying, a small prayer entered my heart.

Dear Lord, please help me figure this out. Give me some kind of sign of what I should do.

I waited a moment, and of course, there was nothing.

"So much for that whole prayer works thing," I mumbled.

I went back to sifting through the stuff. There were more love notes, mementos from special times in our lives. I hadn't realized that Clark had kept all this stuff. I had gone through just about everything when I spotted a long white envelope I'd never seen before. I picked it up and saw a postmark from two days ago.

I glanced at the return address: Gilman Adoption Agency. My heart quickened as I turned the letter over and tore it open. I pulled out a piece of paper and began reading.

Dear Mr. and Mrs. Graham,
It is our extreme honor to tell you that we have located an older child in need of a home. With your preliminary paperwork, everything has been approved and we'd love for you to come meet eight-year-old Franklin. We'd love to arrange this meeting at your earliest convenience. Franklin would love to meet you and I think you guys are going to adore him. Please call my office to schedule.

Sincerely,
Scott Murchin
The Gilman Adoption Agency

The letter trembled in my hand. A picture was attached to the back of Franklin's data sheet. The boy was missing a front tooth, but he grinned like he was the happiest child in the world. He wore a Houston Astros T-shirt, and though he looked a little malnourished, he didn't appear to have a care in the world.

He looked like the child I'd always dreamed I'd have.

I had lost everything. My baby. The ability to have children, my mother, my marriage, and now that I was coming to terms with that, God wanted to send this precious little boy into my life? What kind of madness was this?

A child.

I'd asked for a sign and I'd gotten a child.

I noticed another handwritten note from Clark at the bottom of the letter. He must have opened the envelope and sealed it back up.

Savannah,
I didn't want to tell you about this because I don't want you to come back to me just for him. I want you to come back to me for us, because you want our marriage. Because you love me. I wanted you to recognize, on your own, that you and I were put on this earth to give this child a home. My prayer tonight and every night is that you will take this as a sign that we were meant to be. All three of us.

Love forever,
Clark

My dream of motherhood was about to come true. But would I go back to Clark just because of a child?

I glanced over at the tattered book that had stopped me from making a mistake. If I had slept with Wilson, the guilt alone would've kept me from going back. Though vengeance had seemed right at the time, it wasn't who I was. And I was grateful that I hadn't crossed that line.

I picked the book up and wondered about its history as I remembered Clark reading verses as he tried to pull me out of my grief. I hadn't purposely opened this book, and yet it had changed my life by reminding me that my broken heart could be healed.

And with that revelation, I knew . . .

I set the book back on the nightstand, then stood and started throwing things into my bag. I was going home . . . not for the love of a child. I was going home for love.

I threw my bag over my shoulder, then headed to the door. I stopped and looked back around Room 316. I'd come here with my eyes closed, blinded by pain. And though the pain was still there, I chose happiness. I knew the road ahead wouldn't be easy, but Clark, Franklin, and I, we were going to see it through.

CHAPTER 13

Forgiveness isn't easy. Sometimes it's more painful than the wound itself.

For some reason the words of my old therapist popped into my head. Probably because I'd been struggling for the past week that I'd been home. I had known that it wouldn't be easy. I hadn't known it would be this hard.

I sat at the kitchen table as Clark cooked my favorite omelet. He was rambling like we were fine.

"I'm so excited about this program," he said as he set a glass of juice in front of me. "Jarvis Christian College is really trying to boost their enrollment. They got a grant and they're working with us to identify candidates. They're giving two of our boys full rides. Unfortunately, I'm having the hardest time finding some kids to take advantage of the opportunity."

I tried my best to be interested. At any

other time I would've been. But staying focused on the future — and not the past — was a struggle.

Clark set my omelet down and studied me. "Am I boring you?"

"No," I said, managing a smile. I told myself each day that, while I didn't have to be happy and giddy, it did no one any good for me to walk around clutching my anger like a well-worn sweater. I remember the therapist telling me that there was a reason the front windshield was bigger than the rearview mirror. The past needed to fade away. "I think it's really good what you guys are doing at the Boys & Girls Club. Who are you going to give the scholarships to?"

"I already have one kid on board, William Johnston. His friends call him Wiz."

"Oh, I remember him," I replied. "He's the little freckled cutie-pie you had over for Christmas dinner one year."

"Yes, him and Trey Ruffin. I wanted Trey because he has the book smarts, but he's kinda just dropped off the radar and I haven't been able to get in touch with him. Wiz is excited, though."

Any other time, I would've relished this quality time, talking about the things we loved. But it's like the devil wouldn't let me focus.

"How are we going to heal?" I finally said, immediately shifting the tone of the conversation.

Clark slid into the seat across from me and took my hand. "I don't know. All I can do is make you the promise that I'm going to do whatever it takes. Pastor Ed wants us to come see him," he said, referring to our minister. "If you prefer that we get a regular counselor, we can."

I thought about it. Maybe we could do that after, but right now it was going to take a whole lot of God to help us get through this.

I lowered my eyes, determined not to cry. Why wouldn't my heart cooperate with my head since I'd made the decision to forgive my husband?

"I don't know how many ways to tell you I'm sorry," Clark said. He'd been apologizing every day since I'd returned home.

I opened my mouth, poised to ask for more details about what had happened between him and Dawn. But something made me pause. Would any answer ever be good enough?

You can't start the next Chapter of your life if you keep rereading the last one.

I smiled as I remembered Clark's words when he'd been trying to convince me to adopt — and I answered each request with a "but the baby we lost . . ."

Instead of asking about the past, I decided on neutral ground.

"Whatever happened to that grant you were getting from the Lawson Foundation to renovate the club?" I asked.

Clark leaned back. "Unfortunately, they wrote us a bad check that didn't clear, and that we can't collect on because they filed bankruptcy."

"That's horrible," I said. "So their debt just gets canceled? How shysty."

Clark pointedly looked at me and replied, "Nah, the foundation does good work. Mr. Lawson has really tried his best." He hesitated. "Just because someone really screwed up once and can't repay their debt doesn't mean they are a bad person and will never be able to get it right in the future. Bankruptcy is about canceling all their debts, giving them a second chance, and hoping they have learned a lesson from their experience."

I stared at him, reading the undertones of his message. After a few moments I replied just as pointedly, "But bankruptcy doesn't allow you to just start over as if nothing happened. You have no credit at all. You can't borrow, you have to be accountable for your

114

actions, showing the court that you are worthy of a second chance."

He didn't blink as he responded. "And anyone who really appreciates that second chance, and the fact that they don't have to live in debtor's prison for the rest of their lives, doesn't mind."

"So, the prisoner should just be set free?" I asked.

"It's the first step to forgiveness," he said. "In fact, that's what forgiveness is. A person might not deserve it, but someone sees fit to give you a second chance, believe in you and give you a fresh start." He stopped beating around the bush as he leaned in. "I thank you for coming back to me, Savannah. Now I pray for a fresh start. I want your heart back, and I'd like you to know that I will guard it until the day I die."

We sat in momentary silence, and I resolved — in that moment — that I would choose the front-view window and not the rearview mirror.

"You know what I'd like?" I finally said, smiling at him.

"What, babe?"

"I'd like to finish breakfast and then go see our son."

That made Clark smile, too. Our adoption wouldn't be finalized for thirty days, but we'd immediately bonded with Franklin, and that little boy had given me more joy than I'd ever thought possible. I wasn't just fighting to heal for me and Clark, I was fighting for that new child. Our son.

"I'd like that, too," Clark said. He popped a piece of bacon in his mouth and held my hand as we continued eating.

Clark was more than his mistake. He was right. Freeing him would set me free.

That thought brought me peace.

■ ■ ■ ■

OLLIE

■ ■ ■ ■

CHAPTER 14

There had to be a hundred people here. At least that's how it felt as I listened to the laughter that filled my house. The sound of my sons arguing on the back patio. My daughter and daughter-in-law in the kitchen, laughing as they baked and shared gossip. And then my grandkids, who ran across the living room as if they had no home training. The only one acting like he had any sense was my grandson Jeremiah, who sat in his usual spot on the end of the sofa, headphones on, drowning out the noise as he played on some handheld video game.

Yes, it seemed like a hundred people were here.

In reality, though, there were only about twenty. But that was more stimulation than my seventy-nine-year-old mind could handle. I longed for the silence that I had been encased in for the past six weeks — before my children decided that they needed to celebrate my birthday today. They just didn't understand. I had no desire to celebrate my birthday anymore, especially since my beloved wife, Elizabeth, died one year ago today. Why my kids had the cockamamie idea that a party on the day I lost my soul mate was the answer to my grief was beyond me.

Stop being a pessimist.

I heard Elizabeth's words in my head. And that brought a smile to my face. She used to always complain about how much of a grouch I could be. I didn't *used* to be that way. Old age had brought with it a shorter temper. Right now, though, if I could just get Elizabeth back, I would never utter a grouchy word again.

"Hey, Dad. You sure you don't want a beer?"

I thought about taking a beer just so that my youngest son, Cole, would quit asking. But while their parents didn't seem to care, I didn't like drinking in front of my grandchildren, especially my grandsons. I wanted to make sure they always saw a good example, since alcohol brought out the worst in people, especially my sons.

"No, thanks," I replied.

"Jeremiah, how long are you going to play

that game?" my oldest son, Charlie, said as Jeremiah continued tapping away at the screen. He kicked Jeremiah's foot when the fourteen-year-old didn't answer. "Boy, do you hear me talking to you?"

Jeremiah removed one headphone from his ear. "Yeah, Dad?"

"Put the game down and go play with your cousins."

Jeremiah stared at his father in disbelief. "My cousins are four," he finally said.

"He's all right," I said, tousling the curly red mop atop his head. Jeremiah was the quiet and reserved one of my grandchildren. He was a loner, who I could tell felt like he didn't fit in anywhere — even with our family. And Charlie didn't make things easier for him. He hated that Jeremiah wasn't an aggressive bully like him, and he constantly gave his son a hard time. "Jeremiah's enjoying quality time with his grandpa," I said.

"You call that quality?" Charlie said, pointing at the TV. "You're watching some show in black-and-white."

"It's *Gunsmoke*. It's a classic," I said.

"You're watching *Gunsmoke* and he's catching Pokémons. Yeah, real grandfather-grandson bonding time," Charlie quipped.

"Are we bothering you?"

Charlie threw his hands up. "Fine. Do

whatever makes you happy."

I looked over at Jeremiah. "This makes us happy, right?"

Jeremiah nodded. "Yep." He put his headphone back on his ear and went back to playing his game.

Charlie shook his head and headed outside onto the deck. I went back to watching TV. The show had just gone to a commercial break when my four-year-old twin grandsons raced through the living room. One bumped into an end table and caused a picture of Elizabeth to topple over, fall to the floor, and the glass to shatter into a million pieces.

"Jacob, Jonathan!" I screamed as I jumped up. Both boys froze in fear. I'd been yelling at them for the past hour, telling them to stop running in the house. But since my daughter Marian was into that New Age "let kids be kids" discipline, the twins didn't listen to anyone.

The outburst caused the women to come running in.

"Oh, my God. What did you boys do?" Marian said.

"They broke Grandma's picture," Jeremiah responded, not looking up from his game.

I stared at the shattered glass as mist

covered my eyes. It was my favorite picture of Elizabeth. She'd picked this frame out on my twenty-fifth birthday.

"Dad, I am so sorry," Marian said as she stooped down to help me pick up the broken glass.

"They broke it . . ." I said as I continued picking up the pieces. The corner of the ceramic frame was cracked beyond repair. I was so upset my hands were shaking.

Marian kept uttering apologies, but other than that, silence had filled the room and the twins looked terrified. If Elizabeth had been there, she would have told them not to worry about it as she cleaned up the mess. But all I could do was shake in anger.

"Dad, it's okay. We'll get another frame," Charlie said.

"We've had this frame for fifty years," I snapped.

Jacob stepped toward me and extended a piece of paper. "I sorry, PawPaw. I drewed you a picture."

"See, he's sorry," Marian said, smiling like everything was okay.

Despite my anger, I took the paper — and then I noticed the scribbled crayons over the words on the page.

"Did you . . . ?"

At that point I noticed torn pages leading

a trail down the hall. "Oh . . . my . . . God." I darted over and picked up the pages — ripped from the Bible that sat on the nightstand in my room.

I raced to my room and saw Elizabeth's Bible on the floor with half the pages haphazardly torn out.

"Oh, boys, what did you do?" Marian asked, appearing behind me.

Once again I fell to my knees as I picked up page after page. And each crumpled and torn page pierced my heart.

Everyone must've followed me to my room because Charlie reached over to touch my shoulder. I snatched my body away. I needed to get out of this place. It was suffocating me. I didn't want all these people in my house. I didn't want these people around me. The only person I wanted, I couldn't have.

I stood and stomped back into the living room, picked up the photo, shook the glass off, then stood and headed toward the door. "Dad, where are you going?" Charlie asked. I ignored him as I grabbed my keys off the table by the door and headed out.

"Dad . . ." Marian said as she, Charlie, and Cole followed me out.

"Come on, this is your party. Don't be like this," Cole said.

"You're getting all worked up for nothing," Charlie said.

I didn't say a word as I clicked the remote to unlock the doors to my 2001 Ford F-150. My pride and joy. The truck Elizabeth had finally broken down and let me get.

Charlie said, "Where are you going?"

Still, I didn't reply. I rolled down my window and put the truck in reverse. Cole jumped in the back to keep me from leaving the driveway.

"Dad, it's your birthday. We're not letting you go," he said.

"Cole, if you don't want to end up in the grave next to your mother, you will get out of my way," I hissed. My chest heaved as I struggled to keep my calm.

"Dad, the twins didn't mean it. We'll buy you a new frame," Marian said.

I just glared at her. That was her solution to everything. Just buy a replacement. Some things couldn't be replaced.

"I'm just going out to clear my head. I'll be back," I finally said, hoping that would be enough to get them to leave me alone.

"How long will you be gone?" Charlie asked. "Yvonne and Mandy are on the way over," he added, referring to his sisters.

He was holding that out as bait. Yvonne was the only one of my kids that I could stomach for more than a couple of hours. She was the only one with an iota of sense.

My first instinct was to tell them that where I was going was none of their business. But when I did get back, I wanted everyone out of my house. And I knew anything other than a "soon" would lead to another twenty minutes of them pleading with me not to leave.

"Soon," I said. "Fifteen, twenty minutes. Go back inside and enjoy yourself. I'll be back."

"You know we all have been worried about you," Marian said. "These emotional outbursts, your sadness . . ."

I should've known that was coming. Ever since Elizabeth died, my children had been complaining about how "different" I was. I lost my soul mate. How did they think I was supposed to act?

"I was doing some research —"

"I'll be back." I cut Marian off before she could finish. She had done two years of community college, but the Internet made her act like she had three medical degrees.

As I pulled out of the driveway, I stared at my family staring at me.

"I'll be back soon," I repeated.

The words danced in my head and I

fought off the urge to add, "Just please be gone when I return."

CHAPTER 15

The gentle tap on the window startled me. I didn't even realize how long I had been sitting in the driveway of my longtime friend's house. We'd been knowing each other since the early seventies, when my construction company remodeled his law offices. I rolled down the window and Bruce stuck his head in.

His brow furrowed. "Hey, big guy. What are you doing?"

"Hey, Bruce," I said.

"How's it going?"

"I'm making it," I replied.

Bruce stood back, studied me, and then said, "I got the bourbon on the deck. Come on."

I rolled my window up, then pulled myself out of the truck and followed my friend up the walkway into his home of thirty-plus years. Bruce was a widower as well, but the only difference was he had long gotten over his lost love and gone through a flurry of women to help him heal. Something I not only had never done, but had zero desire to ever do.

"So, what's going on? What brings you to my house, and on your birthday at that? Happy birthday, by the way. But why are you sitting here in my driveway? Just sitting there like an old girlfriend stalking me." He winked as he dropped some ice cubes into a small glass and then poured a drink. "I looked out of the window and thought you were Betty Jean Boiling. She's been after me for weeks."

"I had to get out of my house," I said, taking the glass and immediately downing the drink. The liquor burned my throat before settling in my stomach. "My sons, daughter, grandkids are all over. It's just all too much."

"I would think you'd like having a house full of folks."

"They just never shut up," I said.

A hearty laugh filled Bruce, and his round belly jiggled as he spoke. "You shouldn't have had that baseball team."

"I only had six kids."

"Only and six don't go together," Bruce chuckled, sliding into his La-Z-Boy recliner. "Have a seat."

I plopped down on the sofa across from him, feeling as if the weight of seven planets was on my shoulders.

"So what's got you so down, buddy?"

I hesitated. I had never really talked to anyone about my feelings after losing Elizabeth. Following her death, I just kind of shut down. I didn't think anyone could understand the depths of the pain I was feeling.

"How did you recover?" I finally asked Bruce. "How are you able to just be so carefree and footloose? Just continue living life? Because I know you loved Laura."

"Oh, I did love her. With all my heart. But Laura died. I didn't," he said matter-of-factly.

"That's just it," I replied. "I feel like I did die. This has been the hardest year of my life."

"But you know Elizabeth wouldn't want you walking around here moping."

"It's been a year, and it still feels like yesterday when I put her in the ground. I'm just tired, Bruce. Tired of walking this earth with this huge hole in my heart."

He nodded in understanding. "I get it. Maybe you need to go out on a date."

I cut my eyes at my friend. That was his answer to everything. A woman. It didn't

130

matter that he was the spitting image of Santa Claus, minus fifty pounds, Bruce kept a smorgasbord of women. But that was his thing, not mine. "Now, you know that's not about to happen."

"Okay. Let me rephrase that. Maybe you need to go find something social to do," Bruce corrected.

I released a heavy sigh. "I just don't have any desire to do anything. My kids think I should go see a psychiatrist."

"What?" Bruce said, as if the mere thought was an abomination. "Come on, buddy. You're really going to go lay on somebody's sofa and talk about what ails you? How crazy is that?"

"I know you're right," I said. "You know I'm not doing that. But I gotta do something."

"You know what you gotta do? Go see Elizabeth and tell her goodbye. A real, I'm-moving-on goodbye. I guarantee you, if you get there and talk to her for a few minutes, and listen to her talk to you, she'll tell you she wants you to move on and be happy."

I thought about what my friend was saying. I visited my wife's grave regularly. I talked to her and often felt that she was talking back. But I'd never asked her what she wanted for me. Maybe she would give me

131

some advice on how to heal.

"Okay. I'm going do that," I announced.

"Good, now here." He extended the bottle toward me. "This bourbon isn't going to drink itself."

We sat and talked for another hour, with Bruce trying to make me laugh, to no avail. Finally, I could tell I was bringing my friend down, so I said, "I have to get going. You're right. I'm going to head by Elizabeth's grave. That's what I need. I need to be with Elizabeth."

Bruce shook his head like I was a lost cause. He stood to walk me to the door. "Ollie, I don't know what you need, but you need to do something because I don't like seeing you like this."

I could only reply with a grunt.

I didn't like seeing me like this. But no matter what I did, I couldn't shake the dark cloud that hung over me.

Chapter 16

The rain had stopped me from going to see my beloved wife, and I had hoped it had been the cue for my children to go home. Unfortunately, when I pulled up in front of my house, all of the cars were still there. I considered flooring the gas and driving past. But the day had been long and I was tired. I stifled my groan, threw my truck into park, and then got out and walked inside.

As soon as the front door opened, the mood in the room instantly shifted. The chatter that had filled it was gone. An uneasy silence blanketed the room as everyone turned their attention toward me.

"Daddy. We're so glad you're back," Marian said, jumping up to greet me. She tried to hug me, but I wasn't in the mood and kept my arms at my sides.

I walked around her and into my living room. "I'm back now. So, y'all can leave. It's getting pretty late." My eyes stopped on my daughter Mandy, who was sitting on the sofa with a worried expression on her face. My youngest daughter, Yvonne, sat next to her, her arms folded, her lips pursed in anger.

"Hey, Daddy," Mandy said. "Sorry I was late for the party. I had to work."

"Hello," I told her, then looked at her sister. "Yvonne, what's wrong?"

I could've sworn she had tears in her eyes. But she didn't say a word as she stood and left the room.

The silence made me frown. "What's going on?"

"Dad, we need to talk to you," Charlie said.

Jeremiah looked at me with unspoken words, and the expression on his face made me uneasy. I was taken aback when he walked over, hugged me, muttered, "I love you," and then went outside on the deck.

I watched him walk out and turned my attention back to the five sets of eyes on me — Marian, Mandy, Charlie, Cole, and Charlie's older daughter, Paige. "Talk to me about what?"

"Can you have a seat?" Charlie said.

I almost protested, but I decided that the sooner I did what they asked, the sooner they would get out of my house. In that

134

instant, I made a mental note to change the locks because I just wanted everyone to leave me alone.

"Dad, we've been talking and we think this thing you're in is not healthy," Charlie began.

I cocked my head and studied my oldest son. He and I had never mixed well. He was WD-40 and I was H_2O. Elizabeth had been the peace in our storm. She kept us from killing each other, especially during his teenaged years. She often said that Charlie was just like me — headstrong and defiant. That's why we butted heads. But Charlie was also the worst of my abusive father. Granted, Charlie's abuse was verbal, and mostly directed at Jeremiah, but he could still be a vile human being.

"And what thing would that be that I'm in?" I asked.

"The depression, Dad," Marian interjected. "We think you're depressed, and we have to say it again, we think you really should go see a psychiatrist."

I stared at my daughter, suppressing the words I wanted to say. Bruce was right. There was nothing in my head that talking to some doctor could heal. There was no cure for a broken heart, and that was the only thing wrong with me.

"I have the number of my therapist and she's very good," Mandy said, finally speaking.

I looked at my privileged next-to-youngest daughter, who spent time with her therapist because she couldn't cope with the demands of motherhood and working a part-time job. I couldn't help but roll my eyes. Both Marian and Mandy had always been spoiled and couldn't handle adversity, so they used therapy as a coping mechanism. The last thing I wanted to do was take advice from someone who had somehow never helped Mandy manage her inability to cope all these years.

Yvonne, who had been our surprise baby when Mandy was ten, reappeared in the doorway. But this time there was no doubt that she was crying. She was the complete opposite of my other children. I could only assume the fact that she'd left the room meant that she didn't agree with whatever it was they were trying to tell me.

"Another thing," Cole interjected, his eyes darting back and forth between his siblings, "we've been thinking, and we want to sell the house."

Cole always had been the crazy one. We had a bout where he was messing around with drugs his freshman year of college. To my knowledge, he was clean now, but obviously those drugs had fried his brain. I'd lived in this house for over fifty years. There was no way I was going to let children I brought into this world kick me out of my home. I owned this house outright, and I'd be damned if my kids would just up and decide they were going to sell it.

"Dad, we really feel like you need to be in a facility." This time it was Marian talking. As if, because she was the bossiest of the bunch, she'd been the designee to convince me that somehow this was a viable idea.

"So let me get this straight. On my birthday — on the anniversary of your mother's death — you come here to tell me you want to sell my house and put me in an old folks' home?" I asked, drawing my words out to make sure I hadn't misunderstood them.

Marian nodded. "We think you have early-onset Alzheimer's . . ."

"There ain't nothing wrong with me!" I shouted. "I'm old, dammit. I may forget things from time to time, but it doesn't mean I have Alzheimer's."

I was so sick of them. I'd gotten lost a few times, mixed up their names (like most parents), and lost my keys a dozen or so times, and Marian had declared that I had early-onset Alzheimer's. The only disease I had was missing-my-wife-and-not-standing-my-kids-itis.

"We think," Marian said, her voice still calm, like she was talking to her terror toddlers, "that your forgetfulness, along with your depression, and the strain of maintaining this house, is just all too much. It's time to let the house — and the strain and pain of it all — go." She put her hand on my arm, as if that simple gesture would make her words less piercing.

"This is all of our home, so this is a decision we did not make lightly. But being here, around all of Mom's stuff, is just contributing to your depression. We actually feel like the change would do you good," Marian added.

I looked at Yvonne. "Are you on board with this?"

"Of course not," she said, her voice cracking.

"It doesn't really matter because she's outvoted," Charlie said, glaring at his baby sister. "She thinks that because she's a nurse, she can take care of you. But she works in the ER. She barely has time for her own child — hence the reason her ex-husband has custody."

"You know what . . . ?" Yvonne said, taking a step toward her brother.

Cole grabbed her arm to stop her as Marian jumped back into the conversation.

"We don't want to fight about this." She flashed a smile at me again. "Daddy, just give it a chance."

"And we're not talking about putting you in any old home, Dad," Charlie added. "It's more like an assisted living facility, where you can be around other people like you."

"Like me?" I snapped. "Do I have the plague?"

"Nooo, Dad," Charlie said, rubbing the bald spot in the middle of his curly hair like he was frustrated and I was being ridiculous. "Other old people."

"Yeah, you can play bingo and you guys can go do old people stuff together," Cole said. "You might even find you a nice companion."

I had to take a moment to figure out how many ways I was going to curse out my son. "Boy, if y'all don't get the hell out of my house," I yelled. "Have you ever known me to play bingo? And I dang sure ain't interested in any companion. Just go!" My patience had gone wherever Charlie's hairline went, and I let them all know it by the way I stomped into my kitchen.

Unfortunately, all of them followed me in.

"We talked to Bert and he's in agreement," Marian said, referring to her older brother, who lived in California.

"I don't care if you talked to the Pope, Jehovah, and the Three Wise Men. I ain't going nowhere!"

"Dad, do not overreact," Marian said. "You're getting older. You're spiraling into this depression and you haven't accepted that we all have to die."

"Grandma lived a good life," my oldest granddaughter, Paige, said. I wanted to ask her why she was even in here in this grown folks' conversation. But since Charlie and his wife had been letting her do what she wanted since she was five, I didn't bother. Besides, there was nothing a nineteen-year-old spoiled brat could say to me anyway.

"And that's what you need to focus on," Marian added. "Mom is gone and we're very sad about it. But you can't stay in that sad place. It's just not healthy."

"I'm gonna ask you all again," I said, taking a deep breath. "I'm tired and I want each and every one of you to leave my house."

They exchanged glances until Marian folded her arms.

"Well, Dad, it's already done," she announced. "I have power of attorney, and the decision has already been made."

"I can't believe this," Yvonne snapped. I don't think I had ever seen my daughter so angry. It was obvious that whatever decision they'd made didn't have her stamp of approval. "Happy birthday, Daddy. I hope you enjoy this gift from your kids." Then she turned and stormed out of the house, slamming the front door on her way out.

I was speechless. Marian had been taking care of all my bills (with my money, of course) since Elizabeth died, but that was because she was always the responsible one. Elizabeth and I had given her power of attorney when Elizabeth was sick, so that she could take care of our financial matters while I took care of the children's mother.

I glanced at my daughter, trying to see what kind of evil had taken over her soul. "When we gave you that power of attorney, we never imagined you would use it to tear my world apart. Your mother would be heartbroken," I said, not bothering to hide the hurt in my voice. How could children who I'd spent my whole life caring for turn on me like this?

"No, she wanted us to take care of you, and this" — Marian motioned around the cluttered kitchen — "no one should live like this."

Yes, my dishes were piled high and dirty

coffee cups lined the sink, but domestic stuff wasn't my thing. Shoot, they'd been here all day. If my kitchen bothered them that much, then they could've cleaned it.

"You shouldn't live like this, in all of this clutter," Marian continued. "That's why we think it's best that you go to an assisted living facility. Some of them are really nice. We'll find one you like. And we know you don't like it, but we have made the decision that this is something that we have to do."

"Over my dead body," I spat.

"Dad, we're really worried about you," Cole said.

"Well, don't worry about me," I said, moving toward the living room. "Just get the hell out of my house."

All of them knew better than to argue with me when I was mad, and I was on a whole other level of fury.

"Come on, Britt," Charlie said to his wife, who had been sitting in the corner in the living room, not saying anything. Her standard MO. I often forgot Britt was in a room, because she was like a Stepford wife. She spoke only when Charlie gave her permission. "Grab the kids and let's go. I told you guys Dad would act like this. We'll talk to him later when he's more rational."

"You don't need to talk to me later!" I

knocked a vase to the floor as I stomped toward the front door and swung it open. "I'm real rational!" I took a deep breath when I noticed Jeremiah standing in the doorway, staring at me with wide-eyed concern. "I'm tired of people trying to dictate my life," I said, my voice now even as I struggled to maintain some semblance of calm. "If I want to mourn my wife for the rest of my life, I will."

"And we think that's not healthy," Marian said, grabbing her purse and taking both boys by the hand.

"I don't care what you think," I replied.

"This isn't over, Dad," Charlie said as he gathered his things to leave. "We're going to have to put you in a home. It's done. We'll go look at some places next weekend."

Mandy walked over and tried to kiss me on the head. I jerked away from her touch. She looked like she was going to cry, but Charlie just shook his head, grabbed his keys, and said, "We'll call you later."

Then all of my Judas children and their offspring followed him out.

They didn't need to call me later. As a matter of fact, it would be just fine if they never called me again.

CHAPTER 17

I had been calling Bruce all night and again as soon as I got up this morning. But Bruce was like me. He had a cell phone only because as a retired attorney, he still did some consulting from time to time and his clients needed to get in touch with him. But outside of work hours, Bruce didn't keep his cell phone on. He wasn't answering his home phone, either, so I was two seconds away from getting in my truck and heading back over to his house.

I decided to try his cell one more time. Thankfully, this time he picked up.

"This is Bruce."

"Hey," I said. "I've been trying to get in touch with you."

He chuckled. "I had a hot date. We went down to the casino. Right after you left, Helen showed up and kidnapped me."

I heard giggling in the background.

"I need to talk to you," I said, cutting him

off before he started going into details about his latest conquest.

"What's going on?" he asked.

"I have a legal question."

"And I have legal answers — for two hundred and fifty dollars an hour," he laughed.

"I'm serious, Bruce."

My tone made him turn professional. "Whoa, buddy, okay. Tell me what's going on." Bruce could be a ball of fun, but when it was time to handle business, he would get real serious.

I rushed the words out. "When I got home yesterday, my kids were here and they announced they were going to sell my home and put me in an assisted living facility."

"What? Are you serious?"

"Dead serious, and they think I'm crazy. They think I have dementia or Alzheimer's or something."

"You got old age," Bruce said without a trace of laughter.

"Exactly. That's what I tried to tell them."

"I mean, you're depressed, but that's understandable."

"I know," I said, pacing back and forth across my living room. A deflated yellow balloon from my birthday celebration drifted in front of me. I lifted my leg, stomped on it, and made it pop. "All I know is they'll have to put me in the ground before I let them put me in a home."

"Okay, calm down, big guy. Give me a minute, Helen," Bruce said, his voice away from the phone. I heard some rumbling as if he was moving around. "Now, tell me," he continued, "why do they think they even have the right to take your home?" He was in his official capacity now.

I sighed as I plopped down in my recliner. "Well, when Elizabeth got sick, we gave Marian a power of attorney so she could handle all of our business affairs."

"So did your POA give her the right to sell your house?" he asked.

"I don't know," I snapped. My temple was throbbing. The lack of sleep, coupled with my rage, had to have my blood pressure elevated. I stood and began the trek around my living room again.

"What do you mean, you don't know?" Bruce asked.

"I just signed the dagblasted thing!" My pacing quickened, as if moving faster would bring me clarity.

It was his turn to sigh. "Now, how long have you been my friend, Ollie?"

"A lifetime."

"And what have I always told you?"

I stopped right in front of the last family photo we'd all taken. Jeremiah was still a baby and sitting in Elizabeth's lap. I was smiling, oblivious to the fact that my kids would one day grow up to stab me in the back. "Always read the paperwork," I replied. "But I didn't think that applied to my own child."

"Well, calm down," he said. "The first thing you have to do is find that paperwork."

"I don't know where that thing is." I moved down the hallway to my bedroom as if being there would help me remember what I'd done with our copy of the paperwork.

"Do you think Marian will give you a copy?"

"Not unless it's in her favor."

Bruce paused like he was thinking. "Well, in order for it to be valid, she has to have it on record. But you need to go find it and see if she has the right to sell your house. I know in some cases a doctor has to deem you not competent, but if you gave her autonomy in terms of rights, then you might be in for a fight."

I fell down onto my bed. I didn't have the strength for a fight, especially against my own children.

"I just can't believe this," I said.

"Neither can I," replied Bruce. "But let me know if you find the POA statement and I'll look over it. I'll be back tomorrow."

Before hanging up, I thanked him and promised to keep him posted. I stopped pacing and tried to think. I couldn't remember what I had for lunch yesterday. How was I supposed to remember where a piece of paper was? Where would our copy of that document be, if we even had one? Then it dawned on me that maybe Elizabeth had put it where we put everything else.

I marched over to the closet. I felt around the top shelf until I found what I was looking for.

I threw the large brown shoebox onto the floor, silently cursing myself and my lack of paying attention all these years. My lackadaisical attitude toward matters pertinent to our home used to drive Elizabeth crazy. But I didn't care to know any of the details required to run our household. I just wanted to bring home my check, turn it over to her, and then go watch *Gunsmoke*. She took care of all things domestic. So it was just a natural extension for her to handle the finances as well.

After a while Elizabeth had stopped fighting me over my disinterest and we fell into a comfortable pattern.

I dug through the box. Our birth certificates and wedding certificate was there,
along with our insurance information, but
no power of attorney.

"Oh, Elizabeth," I moaned as I buried my
head in my hands. "Why would they do this
to me? To us, because this is our history."

After Elizabeth died, Marian had really
stepped up to the plate and taken over
where her mother had left off. I'd been so
grateful. I just never had any idea that she
would betray me like this. And I'm sure
Elizabeth didn't, either.

I picked up the box that held all of our
important papers and began stuffing everything back in. I stood and walked back to
the closet where we'd kept these papers
stored for the past thirty years. When I went
to place the box back on the shelf, I noticed
another box with pictures sticking out. I
pulled it out and began sifting through it.

The baby pictures of our children brought
a smile to my face. I fingered the black-and-
white photo of Elizabeth and me standing
in front of our house. It was marked June
12, 1963. We had been so proud to get this
home. I'd worked overtime at the plant for
two years to get the money for the down
payment. And I'd toiled over the years to
pay it off. I'd gotten into the construction

business so that I could figure out how to remodel and expand the house myself. I loved this house, not just because of the sweat and blood that I had put into it, but because it signified my life with Elizabeth. And just like that, it was going to be snatched away . . . just like Elizabeth had been snatched away.

My gaze drifted over to the torn pages from Elizabeth's old Bible. I don't know what happened, but a heaviness overcame me and I did something I hadn't done before. Something I hadn't even done on the day she died — I sobbed and sobbed and sobbed.

"Oh, Elizabeth. I miss you so."

I don't know how long I sat there crying as if I'd just this moment lost Elizabeth. I wanted this nightmare to be over. How could you love a person so much that when they died, you felt like a piece of you had died as well?

Do you, Ollie Lane Moss, take this woman, to have and to hold?

My mind drifted back to the vows we'd taken before Elizabeth's uncle, a Methodist minister. From that day on, I called her my rib. How did a person live without their rib?

In sickness and in health?

Thoughts of Elizabeth caused the tears I

had been so adept at keeping at bay to flow until my tear ducts had run dry. I sat in a nostalgic cloud for a few minutes until I had my answer.

. . . Till death do you part?

How does a person live without their rib? They don't.

CHAPTER 18

The gravel crinkled underneath my tires as I navigated down the long, winding path that led to the back of the cemetery. I could navigate this path in my sleep. I'd come here so many times. My truck could get here on autopilot.

I'd been driving around Houston for the past three hours — just driving and thinking. As always, Elizabeth clouded my thoughts, but for some reason the image forefront in my mind was the first time that we met.

I watched in awe as Max Porter walked with confidence toward the new girl. She wasn't exactly new. She'd been at our school all week. She was the most beautiful girl most of us in the small town of Sealy, Texas, had ever seen. And every boy in school wanted her, including me. I wanted to speak to her, but I had yet to get up the nerve, and when I saw Max, who had been out on a football injury, saunter over toward her, I knew I would never stand a chance.

"Hello, pretty lady," he said. "I'm Max, the star quarterback."

She raised an eyebrow.

"So, your name is Max The Star Quarterback?"

I couldn't help but snicker. Max wasn't fazed, because he replied, "Nope. It's just Max, and I'm the star quarterback. But you probably already know that."

"Actually, I don't," she said. "Excuse me," she added, trying to step around him.

My heart tightened. There had to be at least fifteen people standing around, since we had just gotten out of school. Max didn't like to be embarrassed and he didn't like rejection. Not that I ever saw anyone reject him. Max usually got what he wanted. And it was obvious right now he wanted the pretty new girl. But she didn't want him.

"Excuse me," she repeated when he jumped back in front of her. "I need to get home."

"Well, I'll walk you," he said.

"No, thank you," she replied.

"So, are you too good for me to walk you home?"

She took a deep breath and pulled her

books even closer to her chest. "Look, Max, that's your name, right?"

"That's right."

"I'm not interested, so, if you will please excuse me."

Her bold confidence made me smile until I saw Max's brow furrow.

"What?" he said. "Did you just try to brush me off?"

"Look, I don't want any trouble," she said. I could tell she was a tad bit scared by his change in demeanor. "I just want to go home."

"Nah, I want to know why you don't want me to walk you home."

She just ignored him this time and walked around him. He grabbed her arm, which caught her by surprise. I could tell she was trying to jerk it away, but he had a strong grip on her.

I don't know where the strength came from. My self-esteem was in the tank because of my abusive father, so when it came to violence, I usually ran the other way. But I jumped my puny fifteen-year-old body next to her and said, "You heard her. Leave her alone."

Max looked at me, paused like he had to make sure he wasn't imagining things, then said, "Aren't you the doofus that sits in the front of the class?"

"Leave her alone," I repeated, this time with a bravado that I didn't really have. He released his grip on her arm and took a step toward me. I balled both of my fists up. For what, I don't know. I had never been in a fight in my life. When my dad beat me, I just cowered. I'd mastered the art of cowering. So right now, there was nothing in me that believed I could beat Max. But I was going to try. I wasn't going to go down without a fight. And Max looked like he was gearing up for one, because he began rolling up his sleeves as he took another step toward me. But the gods must have been on my side that day — or really, Mr. Lewis, our high school principal. Because he stepped to us just as Max was about to haul off and punch me.

"Max, I know you're not causing any more trouble. You know one more strike and you are off the football team altogether," Mr. Lewis warned.

That struck fear in Max, because he backed down quickly.

"Nah, Mr. Lewis. We were just messing around."

Mr. Lewis looked at me and said, "Is that true, son?"

I glared at Max. "Yes," I said, not taking my eyes off my nemesis.

Max looked at me like he was relieved I

hadn't gotten him in any trouble.

"Well, good," Mr. Lewis said. "You fellas run along."

I didn't relax until both Mr. Lewis and Max had rounded the corner and were out of sight.

I felt the air release from my body once I could no longer see Max. And the new girl, who I had forgotten all about, said, "Thank you. I've never had anyone take up for me before."

"M-my pleasure," I said. I pushed back all the nervous bubbles in my stomach and said, "I'm Ollie Moss."

She smiled as she extended her hand. "I'm Elizabeth Waters." Her smile widened even more as she said, "Would you like to walk me home?"

That memory made my heart smile. I walked Elizabeth home that day and every day thereafter. We became inseparable. I didn't have to worry about Max because two days after our incident, he'd gotten in trouble and his mother had sent him to the Army. And Elizabeth and I began our life together.

That had been in 1954. Elizabeth and I had married five years later. She stayed while I went off to fight in the Vietnam War. She'd waited on me and had taken care of our two boys — Charlie and Bert — until I was discharged because of an injury.

Elizabeth had been my life and now that she was gone, I questioned everything about my life. No, now that she was gone, my life wasn't worth living.

I pulled my truck into park in front of the headstone where my beloved wife was eternally resting. The vibrating of my phone caused me to look down. Yvonne's name glared across the screen of my cell. I hated these contraptions. My kids had insisted I carry one, but I liked it back when people couldn't get in touch with you. When they had to wait to talk to you until they could reach you.

Only because it was Yvonne, I picked the phone up.

"Hey, baby girl," I said.

"Hi, Daddy," she replied. "How are you?"

"You know I'm not happy." Yvonne was in the perfect position as a nurse. She was caring and sensitive. And the only one of my children who was always concerned with how I felt.

"I know," she said. "I'm sorry I left early. I just . . . We've just been fighting about this for a while."

I wondered how long my children had been secretly talking behind my back about putting me in a home.

"Everyone outvoted me. But Daddy, you can come stay with me. I'll take care of you."

A warm smile filled my heart. "Thank you, sweetheart, but I'll be living in my own house until the day they put me in the ground. Where are you headed?"

"You remember my best friend, Savannah?"

"Yes, the reporter?" I wondered if she agreed with her siblings that I was getting forgetful. She'd been friends with Savannah forever, so of course I would remember her.

"Yes. Well, she's going through some personal issues and I'm trying to help her. I'm on my way over there."

"Oh, okay," I said, not asking any questions only because I couldn't take on the weight of anyone else's tragedies.

"Where are you?" she asked.

"At the cemetery to see your mama."

She was quiet. Then, "Tell her I love her."

"She knows."

"I love you, too, Daddy. And I'm so sorry."

"It's okay, Mandy." I choked back the heaviness in my throat.

Another silence filled the phone. "It's Yvonne, Daddy," she said.

I rubbed my temples. Of course I meant Yvonne. Shoot, I was just getting mixed up

158

from the stress of everything.

"Sorry, that's what I meant. But I need to go."

"Can I come by and take you to lunch this week? I'd rather have my own private birthday celebration. Jeremiah asked if just the three of us could go out somewhere."

"Sounds good," I said.

We exchanged goodbyes and I sat in the car for a moment. I know thinking this was probably bad, but Jeremiah and Yvonne were the only ones I would miss from my family when it was time for me to join my Elizabeth. With the exception of Yvonne, my children were entitled pompous brats who were raising entitled pompous brats, well, except for Jeremiah. Don't get me wrong. I knew that they loved me, and I loved them — but they were still brats. Jeremiah reminded me of myself at that age. Maybe that's why we were so close.

I got out and made my way up to my wife's grave. I sat in front of it, cleaning off the wilted flowers from my last visit, two weeks ago. I filled her in on the birthday party and what the kids were trying to do. After sitting in silence for a few minutes, I finally said, "I miss you so." And then my next words were unexpected: "I'm ready to be with you."

I waited to hear my wife's voice telling me otherwise, telling me "No, it isn't time." Admonishing me for even thinking such thoughts.

But there was nothing.

A plane buzzed overhead. A car honked in the distance. But outside of that, there was nothing.

I took the silence as Elizabeth agreeing. She was ready for me, too. The thought brought me an undeniable sense of peace.

I stood, genuinely smiling for the first time since I'd put Elizabeth in the ground. I was more sure now than ever before. I knew exactly what I needed to do.

CHAPTER 19

I stood at the counter and looked from one end to the other. I had no idea what was the difference between any of these pieces of metal, and it didn't matter to me what kind of gun I got as long as it fired a bullet that could end my misery. That would make the gun perfectly fine with me.

"May I help you?" the man working behind the counter said.

I shifted uneasily. I don't know why I was nervous. Probably because I had never owned a gun in my life. Though I was born and raised in Texas, and came from a family of hunters, I'd never been interested in guns.

"Yeah, ah, wh-what do I need to do to get a gun?" I stammered.

"Is it for protection or sport?" he asked. "That'll determine what type of gun will be best."

"It's to shoot," I replied. I leaned over and tapped the glass, pointing to a small chrome handgun with a black handle. "Matter of fact, just give me that one."

He began unlocking the cabinet. "That one is perfect," he said. "It's one of our best-sellers. It's a Smith & Wesson SW22 Victory. It's a solid weapon, but it's also engineered for superb accuracy and ease of use."

I wanted to tell him to spare me the sales pitch and just give me the gun.

He laid the weapon on the counter. "And you're in luck because this one is on sale, too."

"I'll take it," I said, without even touching it.

"Don't you want to get a feel for it?" he asked.

My expression must've been my answer, because he said, "Well, fine." He slid a paper toward me. "I just need you to fill out a firearms transaction form. And unfortunately, you won't be able to pick it up till Monday because the computer that we use to check backgrounds is down and the office is closed on Saturdays, so I can't do a manual check."

"Monday?"

"Yeah, usually it's instant, but this is the bad side to technology." He had the nerve to laugh.

"I can't wait till Monday!"

The man raised an eyebrow at me. "Well, Texas law requires that I do a background check on you. You can't get a gun until I've run that."

"But I need it today," I snapped.

He pulled the gun back toward him. "Well, I'm sorry, sir. I don't know what to tell you."

I didn't have time for this. I had stopped at the ATM on the way to this gun shop — which I only knew about because I'd passed it once when I got lost trying to pick Jeremiah up from school. So I peeled off three one-hundred-dollar bills and slammed the money on the counter.

"Just give me whatever gun this will buy, please."

The man looked around, and I thought he was going to take the money. But then he pointed back at a sign over his shoulder.

"You see that? Texas law requires a background check," he repeated. "I can't lose my license. Not only that, I could go to jail."

"Okay. Fine." I peeled off two more hundred-dollar bills and put them on the counter. It's not like I'd need any of this after today.

He was fighting with himself. "Can't do it," he finally said as he pushed the money back toward me. His eyes made their way over my shoulder to a young black teen who had just come into the shop. "Sorry, I can't help you," he said to me, though his eyes stayed on the teen. "Whatcha need, young fella?" he called out.

The teen looked uneasy, then said, "Nothing . . . I was . . . I was just looking." Then he turned around and left the shop.

The store clerk shook his head. "I know these thugs aren't trying to rob me," he said. "The last ones that tried ended up paralyzed for life."

"What would make you think he was trying to rob you?" I asked.

The man leaned in and lowered his voice, even though it was just him and me in the store. "He has on a hoodie. Who wears a hoodie in the middle of the day?"

I thought back to my grandson and how he always had a hoodie on. And I wondered if this man would find my grandson a threat. I shook away that thought and said, "So, you can't help me at all? I'm not a criminal or anything. I just really need a gun."

"Sorry, mister. I wish I could," he said, standing upright. He placed the gun back in the case. "I can take your application and you can come back on Monday — Tuesday just to play it safe."

I snatched my money back off the counter and headed outside. What was I going to do now? I'd been prepared to execute my plan, and I'd never dreamed it would be difficult to get a gun. I thought about Bruce. I was sure he had one, but no way would he let me borrow it given the state of mind I'd been in lately.

I was about to climb back into my truck when the teen who'd been in the store approached me. He was still wearing his hoodie, but I wasn't the least bit scared, even though he looked like he was up to no good. I don't know if that's what happens when you're ready to die, but I just said, "Hello, how are you?"

The way his eyes darted around, I had no idea what he was about to do. Maybe he was a robber. Good. Then he could shoot me and save me the trouble.

"Yeah, I, uh, I saw you were looking for a piece," he whispered.

"A piece of what?" I said, frowning.

The nervous way he was looking around told me he definitely wasn't a robber. "A piece. A gun."

I shook my head. "Yeah, but it's some stupid law about a background check and his system is down," I muttered. "Now I gotta try to find another gun shop."

"No, you don't," he said. "What kind of piece? I mean what kind of gun do you want?"

I raised an eyebrow. "One that shoots."

"How much you trying to spend?" he asked.

"I just need a little something." So, this is why he was looking nervous. He was illegally selling weapons.

"You ain't trying to kill no old ladies or trying to rob nobody, right?" the teen asked me.

I frowned in confusion. "So you're a gun dealer with a conscience?"

"Look, old man," he huffed. "Do you want the piece or not?"

He lifted his jacket and revealed a small black pistol. "Don't worry. Ain't no bodies on it."

I had no idea what that meant. His eyes darted around, and I could tell he wanted to hurry up and complete this transaction. I guess my hesitation bothered him, because he dropped his jacket.

"Look, either you want it or you don't."

"Yes, yes," I said. "I'll take it." I reached into my pocket and pulled a hundred-dollar bill out.

"Nah, man. Three hundred. Like what you were about to pay in there."

I debated arguing with him. But this time tomorrow, money wouldn't matter to me. I handed him the whole five hundred dollars.

He looked at me, stunned after he took the money. "Wow."

"Can I have the gun now, please?"

He put it in my hand, and before I could say another word, he had taken off around the corner. I dropped the gun in my jacket pocket, then climbed into my truck. I was that much closer to being with my dear Elizabeth, and that thought made me smile.

I was about to start my truck when my cell phone rang and my grandson's name came across the screen. I pressed ignore just because if I heard his voice, I might change my mind, and I didn't want to change my mind.

I started my truck and headed to do what I needed to do.

CHAPTER 20

Things had drastically changed at the Markham Hotel.

This was the place where I'd begun my life with Elizabeth (both with the proposal and the marriage), so it was fitting that it would be the place where I'd end it. It was actually prophetic that the Markham was the only hotel still standing in Houston from the 1940s. Granted, it had been modernized to the point that it almost looked like a new hotel. Thankfully, it still had its historic feel.

Elizabeth and I had come back here for our twenty-fifth anniversary. But we hadn't been here in years. Life had gotten in the way. Oh, how I wished that I had brought her back here, at least once a year.

I made my way inside to the front counter. As I waited for the two people in front of me to complete their business, I tried to recall the room number that Elizabeth and

I had spent our honeymoon night in.

Room 572. It came to me with a nostalgic smile. Elizabeth had always said that was our lucky number. Two years ago, she'd even won three thousand dollars playing those numbers on the Pick 3.

"Good evening, and welcome to the Markham Hotel," the cheery clerk said to greet me. "How may I help you today?"

"I need a room," I said, praying that they weren't sold out. I hadn't thought about that until this very moment.

My heart sank with relief when she said, "King-size or double?"

"A king," I replied. "And I'd like Room 572," I said. "No, I need Room 572," I corrected.

The clerk tapped her computer screen and then her eyebrows furrowed. "I'm so sorry, but 572 is occupied."

"No," I repeated. "I need 572."

Sympathy filled her face as she said, "I'm so sorry, sir. Room 572 is occupied. And it looks like they're here all week."

There had been very few times in my life that I wanted to cry. But this was one of them. It seemed like everything that could work against me was working against me. "I need 572."

"I'm so sorry," she repeated. "Is there

another room that will do?" She clicked on the screen. "We have 316 available. It has an amazing view overlooking the courtyard, where one of the oldest trees in Houston is preserved."

I wasn't in the mood for a history lesson or another room. "I don't want . . ." And then it dawned on me — 316. March 16 was Elizabeth's birthday, and we were married underneath that tree. This was divine intervention.

"Yes," I exclaimed, "I'll take 316." I whipped out my credit card and driver's license and waited for her to check me in.

Within minutes, I was standing in the entryway to the room. Room 316 would be just fine. I surveyed the interior. It was nothing like it was when Elizabeth and I had saved all our money to afford the thirteen-dollar-a-night rate. I smiled as I thought of how we had saved for four months to enjoy a week at this hotel. My heart skipped a beat as I went and peered out the window. With the remodeling, I was sure the huge oak tree, which we'd stood under and exchanged vows, would have been decimated with modernization. But the front desk clerk was right — the tree stood with what looked like a historical marker in front of it. I couldn't read what it said, but I figured the tree was the reason for the sign.

My heart warmed at the memories of Elizabeth and me with her father beaming by her side, and my mother struggling through it all, mortified that we weren't getting married in a church, but trying to remain supportive. I chuckled as I remembered her reaction when I first told her that we were getting married at a hotel.

"That's blasphemy," she'd said. "You're going straight to hell. What God has put together, let no man take apart. If you're not standing before God, how can you put a stamp on your marriage?"

"Mom, I thought you were always the one that said God was everywhere."

I'd stumped her with that one, because she just muttered, "That marriage won't last," as she walked off.

I reached my hand to the window as if I could touch the tree. Not only had we lasted, we were time-tested. And now it was time for us to be together again.

Chapter 21

Granddad, where are you? Call me.

The text was from my grandson, followed a series of calls — all of which I ignored.

"I'm sorry, Jeremiah," I said as I turned my phone off and set it on the desk. I pulled open the desk drawer and placed the gun inside until I was ready for it.

I'd swung by my house and grabbed a few items before I went to the gun store. I'd wanted to get Elizabeth's favorite suit. A gray pinstripe that made me itch, but she loved me in it. She'd picked it out in Woolworth's in 1977. She'd bought me plenty of suits over the years, which I seldom wore because I worked in construction until I retired and then usually wore khakis and a polo to church. I might have had nicer suits, but this suit was special.

I pulled it out of my bag and carefully laid it across the bed, along with a purple tie that Jeremiah had given me for Christmas last year. This tie was special, too, because Jeremiah had used his own money to have it made with a U.S. Army medallion on it. I smiled as I thought of how proud he'd been to present that tie to me.

I showered, dried off, then turned on the TV as I got dressed. Elizabeth and I used to watch *Let's Make a Deal* every evening before the five o'clock news, so I wanted to end things doing something she and I used to love.

It took me longer than normal to put my clothes on. I guess it was because I was just moving slow, because I wasn't nervous. In fact, I was ready.

I released a heavy sigh after I surveyed myself in the mirror. The suit, which I hadn't worn in at least two years, was a little snugger than I remembered. But otherwise, it was fine.

I slowly ran the comb through my thinning hair, patting it down until I was sure that it, too, was just as Elizabeth used to like it.

I moved back over to the window, a nostalgic smile across my face. There's something about knowing today is your last day on earth that brings a sort of peace. You would think as I stood there, looking out into the courtyard, my mind trying to paint a mental picture of my wedding, that I'd be sad.

But knowing that I was moments away from joining Elizabeth, I felt happy and at ease. The joy of no longer having pain front and center in my thoughts. All that was left now was to leave a note for my family. Honestly, I'd rather have just done what I had to do. But my family was dysfunctional enough. I didn't want to add to the drama. I had a will that would settle the disputes over what little possessions and money I had. But I hadn't told anyone where that was, and I wanted to minimize the fighting after I was gone. I left the window and went over to the desk, pulled out the hotel's note-pad, and began writing.

To my dearest family,
I know you may never understand my decision today. I hope that it does not cause our family to erupt in turmoil. For years I have lived doing what's best for you all. Now I have to do what's best for me. You all were right about one thing — I have been depressed, sad, and living in a world that I have no desire to be a part of. The only thing that I want is to be with my wife again. I don't expect any of you to understand my decision.

But this last year has been the most miserable year of my existence, and I do not wish to live another year in that pit of despair.

Do not weep for me, as I have lived a good life. My will can be found in the back of my closet in a brown shoebox on the top shelf. Please honor it accordingly.

Until we meet on the other side,
forever my love,
Dad.

I thought about leaving a snide remark about how they were free to sell my house now, or mentioning how them trying to push me out of my house was the wind that pushed me over the cliff. But this would hurt enough. No need to leave a trail of guilt.

I needed an envelope so that the letter would be sealed until whoever found me could take it to them. I opened the desk drawer, found a hotel envelope, then placed the letter inside.

Chapter 22

It was time. I had strolled down memory lane for as long as I could. It was time to carry out what I had come here to do. I had showered and changed into my suit and was ready to meet my maker . . . and dance with my wife.

I positioned the letter on the desk, then turned to study my reflection in the beveled mirror. I wasn't a bad-looking guy. My powder-white hair and Socratic beard should've made me look older, but I didn't have the timeworn skin of most men my age. Yet I bore what people couldn't see — a weatherworn heart. They couldn't see that my soul was empty.

I stood and straightened my tie. An image of my children flashed through my head. I said a quick prayer that I was doing the right thing, that I wouldn't create any more chaos in their world. I also wondered whether I should write a note for Jeremiah. Something encouraging because, while the others would be sad, my grandson would be heartbroken.

And yet that thought wasn't enough to make me change my mind.

Deciding against a note, I walked over, pulled the gun out of my duffel bag, then sat on the edge of the bed. I had just placed the gun in my lap when a book on the nightstand caught my attention.

I leaned over to pick it up. The tattered pages . . . the chipped gold embossment. This looked exactly like the Bible that had been in Elizabeth's family. The one she'd been frantic about on our wedding day.

If I didn't know better, I would think this was her book . . . lost here all those years ago.

"Ollie, come quick! Elizabeth needs you!"

The sound of Elizabeth's maid of honor, Carol, jolted me out of my seat, where I'd been nervously smoothing out my pant leg as I prepared to marry the love of my life.

"What's wrong?" I said, panicked. Images of my soon-to-be wife changing her mind about marrying me ran through my head. No. Elizabeth loved me. She wouldn't be backing out.

"I don't know," Carol said. "Her father

177

showed up and said something, and Elizabeth just lost it."

I took off down the hall to Elizabeth's dressing room. I pounded on her door.

"Elizabeth, dear. Are you okay?"

"No," she cried through the door.

"I'm coming in," I said, pushing the door open.

She slammed it back closed. "No, you can't see me."

"Just take my hand," I said. "Please."

She cracked the door and I slid my arm through. I waited, my heart racing until I finally felt her touch.

"Sweetheart, talk to me."

"It's my Bible."

"Your family Bible?"

"Y-yes. It's gone," she whimpered.

"What do you mean, gone?"

Elizabeth had been so excited about the minister marrying us with a Bible that had been in her family for generations. Her mother, grandmother, and great-grandmother had all been married with that Bible.

"Daddy said it's missing. What are we going to do?"

My mind was racing. I knew the Bible was important to Elizabeth, but there was no way I was going to let this special day pass by because it had come up missing.

"Sweetheart, my mother always says it's not the book that matters. It's what's in the book. And what's in the book is in our hearts."

Silence came from the other side of the door and my heart skipped. Finally, Elizabeth said, "You're right. It's in our hearts."

We'd moved forward, and the next day I'd gone out and bought her a new Bible, to begin a new tradition. That's the one my grandchildren had ripped to shreds.

I continued running my finger along the frayed edges of the book in my hands. I flipped it open and smiled at where it landed.

The book of Jeremiah, Elizabeth's favorite passage. The day our grandson Jeremiah was born, Elizabeth held him in her arms and recited the verse. *For I know the thoughts that I think toward you . . .*

A chill shot through me as I heard a voice finish the verse.

. . . thoughts of peace, and not of evil, to give you an expected end. It sounded as if the voice was right there in the room with me. I slammed the book shut and set it back on the nightstand.

I shook off the eerie feeling buzzing in my ears. My nerves were getting the best of me. Opening to that chapter had been purely coincidental. I had come to the Markham on a mission, and I couldn't let anything derail my plan.

I took a deep breath, nervous about pulling the trigger. No more delays. I put the gun to my head and started muttering, "One . . . two . . ."

Suddenly, there was a knock on the door. "Housekeeping," the voice called out.

I jumped up. "Are you serious?" I muttered. Why the heck did they have a Do Not Disturb sign if they were going to disturb you? I ignored the voice and was just about to put the gun back to my head when I heard the door open.

"Housekeeping," she called out again.

I threw the gun under a pillow and raced toward the end of the bed. "It says 'Do Not Disturb' for a reason!" I yelled. I must have frightened her.

"I'm so sorry. I thought you were out . . ." she said, quickly closing the door.

"That's why the Do Not Disturb sign is there!" I barked.

"I'm sorry. So, so sorry," she said from the other side.

I muttered silent curses and then shook away my irritation. I didn't want to spend my last moments on earth angry and worked up.

I headed back to my spot on the bed, determined to get this over with before there were any more interruptions. I pulled the gun from under the pillow and had just positioned myself against the headboard when I noticed the anchor on the five o'clock news, which had just come on. But today, what was on the screen caused me to jump up and unmute the TV. The camera zoomed in on my son, Charlie, who was clutching a tearful Britt. They were looking at something as the anchor talked over the video of them.

". . . Police are on the scene, trying to talk the young man down," the anchor said.

I remained frozen, my eyes riveted to the TV and the camera as it panned from Charlie to Britt to a figure on the bridge. I had to sit down so I didn't lose my balance when I saw the purple hoodie that Jeremiah always wore.

The anchor for Channel 26 continued, "Savannah Graham is live at the scene with an update. Savannah, what's the latest?"

Savannah was one of my favorite reporters, not just because she was Yvonne's best friend, but because she was genuinely good at what she did.

"Melissa," Savannah began, "authorities are trying to talk the young man down. Witnesses say the boy reportedly jumped out of a car when it came to a stoplight here at Highway 59 and Shepherd. He took off running and came here to the overpass on Interstate 59. He was able to climb over the fence and is now on the other side, suspended over the highway. Authorities are in the process of shutting down the highly trafficked freeway."

All thoughts of anything I was about to do evaporated, especially when the camera zoomed in on a panicked Charlie pleading through the fence to Jeremiah.

I couldn't hear what he was saying, but I could see the despondent look in my grandson's eyes. I recognized it because I bore it myself.

My heart raced as I noticed the rush-hour traffic. There were some cars whose drivers must have been oblivious to what was going on, because they whipped by.

I slid the gun under the mattress, grabbed my keys, and bolted out of the room, praying I could make it to Jeremiah before it was too late.

CHAPTER 23

The only other time I'd felt fear like this was when I'd held my dear Elizabeth's hand and watched her take her last breath. I was mortified at the sight of my grandson teetering on the bridge, overlooking Highway 59. Thankfully, they'd stopped traffic below so there were no cars. I'd had to take back streets to get here and left my truck illegally parked in someone's driveway.

The firemen had set up a trampoline under the bridge, I guess to catch him if he fell. I wanted Jeremiah to see me, because maybe I could get through to him.

"Dad! Thank God you're here," Charlie said when I approached the scene. Though they'd been near Jeremiah when I first saw them on the news, they were now standing behind some police tape about a hundred feet away.

Britt was a nervous wreck, sobbing and moaning, "My boy, someone save my boy."

I ignored her as I turned to Charlie.

"What happened?"

"We were fighting as we were headed to pick up Paige, and the next thing I knew, he jumped out the car at the stoplight," Charlie said. "Now, the cops won't even let me try to talk to him."

"My boy . . . My boy . . ."

I wanted to tell Britt that she was just making everything worse, but I kept my focus on Charlie.

"What did you say to him?"

"How do you figure it was me?" Charlie asked, then another police car sped up on the scene. "Can you believe this mess Jeremiah has gotten us into?" Charlie barked. "It's all on the news. This is just ridiculous."

I wanted to shake some sense into my son, get him to focus on the real issue at hand, but he'd have to wait.

"Please, may I get through?" I asked the police officer standing in front of the yellow tape.

"No, sir. No one can go in yet," the officer said.

"I'm his grandfather. I may be able to talk to him," I pleaded.

The cop looked over at another officer who was looking our way. The other officer nodded, and the cop in front of the tape stepped aside to let me through.

I took measured steps toward the wire fence. Jeremiah had his fingers intertwined in the fence from the other side as he stood on the tiny edge of the bridge, facing away from me. One wrong move and he would plummet thirty feet.

"Jeremiah, what are you doing?" I gently said.

Tears were streaming down my grandson's face, and my heart dropped as he looked at me but didn't say anything.

"Son, talk to me," I said.

He didn't reply, just continued crying. Finally, he said, "I can't take it anymore, Grandpa."

"I know." I nodded. "I know firsthand how hard it is for you."

I took a step closer, then motioned to the officers nearby to let me do this as they moved in like they were about to stop me. Thankfully, they backed down.

"No, you don't know what I'm going through," Jeremiah said. "I'm bullied at home. I'm bullied at school, and I'm just sick of it. I'm tired of living."

"I know, son. Me too. I was sick of living, too."

"Huh?" he said, looking back at me in

185

confusion.

I got right up on the fence and was able to touch his hands through the wires.

"I know you might not be able to understand, but just a few minutes ago, I was about to do what you're doing. Seeing you in distress saved me."

Confusion spread across his face. "You were about to jump off a bridge?"

"No, but I was about to take my own life."

His eyes widened in horror. Then, he said, "You're just saying that."

I shook my head. "Have you ever known me to lie?"

He thought for a moment, then said, "No."

"You have been calling me, right?" I continued.

"Yes, you haven't been answering."

"Just a few hours ago, I was where you are, despondent. I felt like life wasn't worth living. And I was prepared to do something about it. I was prepared to die."

"You were really going to leave us?" Jeremiah asked.

I nodded in shame. "I just wasn't happy. I wanted to die. But driving here in a panic, I thought about you leaving me and I realized all the people I'd hurt if I had done that." I fought back my tears. "I'm going to be real hurt if you leave me, Jeremiah."

At that point a fireman eased up on the side of me. He had a long, thick rope in his hands. We exchanged unspoken words. "Can this nice fireman throw the rope over and pull you to safety?" I asked.

Jeremiah looked at me, then over at his parents, then at the crowd that had gathered.

"Grandpa, I'm so sorry."

"It's okay. Just let him toss the rope over so he can pull you to safety."

Jeremiah looked back down onto the freeway and fear finally crept up on his face. He gripped the fence tighter and said, "Okay."

I nodded for the fireman to step up. I kept caressing Jeremiah's fingers through the fence. "You know, I was sad because I didn't have your grandmother, but I have you. And you have me."

The firefighter tossed the rope over.

"What's your name, son?" the firefighter said.

"Jeremiah."

"Okay, Jeremiah, wrap the rope around your waist and tie it into a knot. Then I want you to climb back over. I'll pull the rope so you don't have to worry about falling."

Jeremiah nodded as the firefighter threw

the rope over the fence. My grandson kept one hand clutched onto the fence and took the other and grabbed the rope.

"Wrap it around your waist, son," the firefighter said.

Jeremiah did as he said, then the firefighter reached through the fence and grabbed the rope.

"Okay, so I have you now. I need to you tie a knot," the firefighter said. "You gotta use both hands, but don't worry. I'm super strong so I'm not going to let this rope go."

Jeremiah paused, then slowly released his grip on the fence. Once he was confident the fireman wouldn't let go, he tied the rope in a double knot around his waist.

"Good job," the firefighter said.

"Jeremiah, we love you," I said. "Don't you worry about —"

Before I could finish, the fireman reached over, grabbed him, and pulled him to safety.

The crowd that had gathered broke out cheering and crying. I rushed to my grandson, took him in my arms, and sobbed with them.

Britt came rushing over, Charlie by her side. "Oh, Jeremiah, why would you do something like that?" she said, smothering him with kisses as he embraced her.

I could tell Charlie wanted to read him

the riot act, but I shook my head in silent retribution. Thankfully, for once in his life, my son listened. He hugged Jeremiah. "You gave me such a scare."

Jeremiah didn't hug him back, and that made my heart sad. Watching my son and grandson, and their damaged relationship, I knew — this was the reason God didn't let me go. This was why I'd stopped to look over the Bible, why the housekeeper interrupted me. To buy time for me to see the news.

Everything happens for a reason, I heard Elizabeth's voice say. Every time I'd get upset because something didn't pan out the way I wanted, she would remind me of that. And now, I knew the reason I hadn't pulled the trigger. I couldn't leave this earth until I'd helped the two men who needed me the most.

Jeremiah tore himself away from his parents and wrapped his arms around me. "I'm so sorry, Grandpa. I'm sorry I scared you."

"Shhh, it's okay," I said, stroking his back.

The paramedics came over and examined Jeremiah. Two police officers talked to Charlie and Britt; the news media shouted out requests for interviews. I saw Yvonne's friend Savannah trying to get to us. But I stayed close to Jeremiah's side and kept them all at bay. We wouldn't be exploiting his pain. I had a new purpose — protect my grandson at any cost.

The day's events had worn on all of us. We were back at Charlie's house, trying to decompress. I knew Charlie wanted me to leave — he'd told me as much on several occasions — but I wasn't going to until I knew Jeremiah was all right.

We'd just eaten dinner when Charlie cleared the table, sat back down, and set his gaze on his son.

"Jeremiah, we gotta talk about what happened today. Why would you do something like that?" he said.

I was grateful that he wasn't going ballistic, so I didn't interject.

Britt sat behind Charlie, looking like the day's events had sucked all of the life out of her and for the first time I realized that her instability made her incapable of supporting her son.

Jeremiah just shrugged, refusing to look his father in the eye.

"You scared a lot of people." He pointed to Britt. "Your mother is still shaking."

"That was so selfish, you little brat," Paige said. Someone had sent her something on social media, and all she was worried about was how everyone was going to think their "family was nutty."

Jeremiah winced, and I realized that Paige had picked up her father's emotionally abusive ways. And Britt, in her fragile emotional state, was no help to any of them.

"You know what?" I said, standing. "I think Jeremiah should come take a ride with me."

"Dad, we're talking to Jeremiah," Charlie said.

"No, you're talking *at* Jeremiah. And after the day he had, that's not what he needs right now."

Charlie slammed his palm on the table, causing us all to jump. "That's his problem. You and his mama are always babying him, making him into a pansy. I'm not raising a weak boy."

"Too late for that," Paige snarled.

"Suicide is for the weak, son. You need to man up —"

"Stop it!" I yelled. "Then count me as weak, too!"

Charlie looked at me in confusion, but I ignored him as I turned to Jeremiah.

"Now do you see why I'm tired?" my grandson said before I could speak. "It's like this every day. I hate it here. I hate them. I hate life. I would be better off dead!"

Britt sobbed. The words caught Charlie off guard, and he stared at his son in shock.

"Let's go, Jeremiah." This time I didn't wait for Charlie to interject. I grabbed my grandson's hand and led him out. I had to go back to the hotel to get my things and check out anyway.

This was a perfect time to get my grandson out of that toxic environment and come up with a plan to remove him permanently.

CHAPTER 24

Silence filled our ride back to the Markham Hotel. I wanted to give Jeremiah time to calm down, and I needed to come to terms with what I should do. I knew that Charlie was bad, but I hadn't fully realized the effect that it was having on my grandson. I was so blinded by my own grief that I was oblivious to my grandson's plight.

I couldn't help but reflect on where I had gone wrong in the raising of Charlie. When he was growing up, I used to blame Elizabeth for babying him. Just like he was blaming Britt now. I supposed that Charlie simply had the worst of both of us in him: my father and me.

It was too late for me to save my son, but I was determined that my grandson wouldn't grow up in a household like the one I grew up in.

"Why are we here, Grandpa?" Jeremiah asked when I finally pulled up to the valet at the hotel.

"Come on." I handed the valet my keys and made my way inside.

"This is the hotel where I was when I saw the news. It has some special meaning," I told him. "It's where I proposed to your grandmother, and where we got married."

"It doesn't look that old," Jeremiah said.

"I know, they've done a lot of remodeling."

Instead of heading up to the room, I made a right in the lobby and headed toward the courtyard. "Come on, let me show you something."

I led Jeremiah out a side door and over to the old oak tree.

"This spot is where your grandmother said she would marry me, and where we later exchanged vows." I thought standing here would make me sad, but it actually made my heart smile.

Jeremiah leaned down and read the historical marker.

"Planted by Mr. and Mrs. Frederick Martin, 1938. Wow."

We stood together in comfortable silence. I felt Elizabeth's presence throughout. And this time I heard her say, *Job well done, my love. Job well done.*

After a few minutes, I said, "Let's head

upstairs so I can get my stuff out of the room."

Jeremiah remained silent as we made our way up in the elevator. Once we reached the third floor, I reached in my pocket and took out the key to open Room 316.

I immediately went to grab the note. At this point I didn't want anyone to ever see it.

"I'm going to use the restroom," Jeremiah said, stepping into the bathroom.

I started gathering my things, then remembered the gun. I raced over to the mattress, reached underneath, and pulled it out. I had just dropped the gun in my duffel bag when I turned to see Jeremiah standing in the doorway, watching me.

"You really were going to do it?" he said. "I thought you had made that up. I —"

I cut him off. "I'm ashamed to say that I was."

"So I guess we both were going to take the coward's way out," he said, his eyes bearing a shame of their own.

I walked over and gripped him by the shoulders. "Don't. Don't ever say that. We weren't cowards. We were despondent. We'd lost sight of what matters. It doesn't matter what almost happened. All that matters is what did happen."

"What if we both had —"

"We're not even going to think about that," I interrupted. "Everything happens for a reason. The housekeeper interrupted me, which gave me time to see you on the news."

"Wow, maybe she was an angel sent to save us both, because if you hadn't come, I had made up in my mind that I was going to jump."

It broke my heart to realize Jeremiah had been so close to death. I also thought about that angel of a housekeeper. I had been so rude to her, and one of Elizabeth's favorite sayings popped to mind: *Do not neglect to show hospitality to strangers, for thereby some have entertained angels unaware.*

I was going to ask about the housekeeper on the way out. Maybe I could give her a tip, though honestly, I could never repay her for what she'd done.

"Let's go, son," I told Jeremiah after I'd gathered all my belongings.

I headed toward the door, but Jeremiah remained by the window.

"You ready?" I asked.

He turned to me. "I don't want to go back there. I don't want to go home."

I paused, then found myself asking, "Your dad doesn't hit you or anything, does he?"

Jeremiah shook his head. "No, but what he does do is a lot more painful. He beats my soul."

I'd never given a lot of thought to verbal abuse, because my father hurt us with his fists so much that we almost welcomed the emotional punishment.

"You know what?" I said after a few more moments of silence. "I've been thinking. Everyone seems to believe that the problem is me living alone. Do you know where I could find a young man, about fourteen, fifteen, who would like to live with me, keep me out of trouble?"

Jeremiah's eyes widened. "Are you for real?"

"I am."

Then just as quickly, dejection made his shoulders slump. "Dad is never gonna go for that."

"Oh, I'll convince him." I didn't know how, but in the last few hours I'd learned that anything was possible. If I couldn't get through to Charlie, I would go through Britt, convince her to finally stand up to her husband.

"Only one condition, though."

"Anything."

"I want both of us to go talk to a therapist. Maybe talking about our issues can do us both some good," I said.

He shrugged. "As long as I can come live with you, I'm good. I'll talk to whoever you want."

At first I thought I'd been spared in order to save Jeremiah, but as we left Room 316, I realized that Jeremiah was spared to save me, too.

ANNA

CHAPTER 25

This was the life I'd envisioned. At least a good part of it anyway. I fingered the photo of my family and smiled. When I'd come to America, my dream had been to create a home for my family, to escape the atrocities of Hidalgo, Mexico, and live a life my parents had been unable to give me.

I guess the best-laid plans don't always go as planned.

When Julio and I had taken this picture, we were proud parents of our fourth child. Our children had been the driving force to create the best life we could. And when Julio died just two months after this photo, I'd tried to carry on the parenting journey alone.

And I'd had a 75 percent success rate.

My three heartbeats made the journey all worthwhile. Alejendro with his angelic dimpled smile and the innocence of his seven years on earth; Maria, who, at nine, managed to find light in the darkest of days; and Miguel, my wise-beyond-his-thirteen-years son who had made me the president of the proud mama club — they were the reason why I worked so hard.

But my fourth child — my oldest, Paco, who had traveled the underground journey to America with Julio and me — was another story.

Paco was in God's hands. That's the only place I could put him.

My eighteen-year-old had left our family for the gang life, and nothing I did could bring him back. I wished that my Julio had been here, because then Paco would've walked the straight and narrow. But Julio had died in a freight accident at work when Paco was just eleven years old. And now, my son was a lost cause.

I was determined to get things right with my other three. Though I still had to work a lot because I was a single parent, I made sure that they got all my time off, that they knew they were a priority in my life and I stayed present in theirs.

We had a few friends here in Houston, but the bulk of our family remained in Hidalgo, in a life that was ravaged with poverty and crime. It was a life that I never wanted my children to know. That's why

Julio and I — three weeks after getting married at age seventeen — had endured the worst of conditions to sneak across the U.S. border. That's why I worked as much as possible at my job as a housekeeper in the Markham Hotel. I took overtime anytime I could, often on the overnight shift just so I could be there to see my kids off to school.

"Mommy, hurry, the zoo is gonna close," Alejandro said.

"*Mi hijo,* it's ten in the morning," I replied, snapping out of my trance and setting the picture down. I headed back into the kitchen to resume packing their lunches for our outing. "The zoo is open all day."

"But I'm ready to go now," he whined.

"Little *niño,* what did I tell you about being patient?" I said, calling him the name that Julio had affectionately given to him when he was still in my womb.

"The patient bird gets the worm," he exclaimed.

"And if you want the worm, you must be what?"

"Patient!" Maria answered for him from her seat in the corner, where she was reading the latest Harry Potter book. My daughter was a voracious reader, and just watching her with her head buried in a book always brought a smile to my face.

203

Alejandro's shoulders sank in defeat. "Okay, Mommy," he said.

"Miguel, are you ready?" I called out to my son, who was back in the bedroom that he shared with Alejandro. I had given Maria my room and I slept on the sofa. It wasn't the ideal situation, but we made do.

"He's playing his video game," Maria said.

I groaned and marched to the back, where Miguel was indeed playing on a PlayStation that I'd won at a work raffle. I had used my last dollar for that raffle and was stunned when I won. But the gamble was worth it because of the joy the games brought to my son's face. He had such a wonderful attitude and was always stepping up to the plate to help with his brother and sister. Miguel was a straight-A student and president of the student council at his middle school.

I fussed at him about these video games, but he made me so proud.

He and his siblings were the reason that I refused to accept any handouts. All I wanted to do was work, raise my family, and keep to myself.

"Miguel, we're going to leave you," I announced.

He leaned to the right, navigating his controller as if he was in the middle of real-life combat. "I'm coming. I'm coming."

"Vámonos."

"Mom," Miguel said, "speak English."

I marched over, turned his game off, then turned to face him. "This is your home. You are an American. But don't ever forget your roots," I scolded him.

"Yes, ma'am," he said, knowing that was one subject where he didn't want to mess around with me.

I was proud of my Mexican heritage, and if conditions had been different in Hidalgo, I would've gladly stayed. But America had been good to us. My children had a life here. A life they could have only dreamed about in Hidalgo.

"Now, *vámonos!*" I told Miguel as I walked back into the living area of our small two-bedroom house, which though it was tattered and in desperate need of remodeling, I'd managed to make a home.

"Come on, children," I said. "Let's go. I have to stop by my job and pick up my paycheck. After we leave the zoo, we can go get ice cream."

"Yay," both Alejandro and Maria said at the same time as they jumped up to follow me toward the door.

"Miguel, wash the dishes while we're gone," I yelled. That was enough to have my son come flying out of his room. He caught up with us just as I was about to close the door.

CHAPTER 26

My children and I had begun walking toward the bus stop when Miguel tugged my arm.

"Mom," he muttered, his eyes fixated on a figure stumbling down the sidewalk.

I stopped in my tracks as my oldest son approached us. He was so thin it brought tears to my eyes. I hadn't seen Paco in five months. We'd had a big blowup the last time he came to visit, because I tried to keep him from leaving to go back into the streets. And in all those months the streets had not been kind to my child.

"Mijo!" I cried, racing over to pull him into my embrace.

He only halfheartedly hugged me back. But I was so happy to see him that I didn't care. I was constantly worried about Paco, but it was a huge relief to lay eyes on him.

"Hey, Ma," he said, diverting his gaze. Even though he looked like he had lost thirty pounds, that wasn't what worried me. My son's usually flushed face was hollow, like he'd danced with the devil and traded his soul.

"Paco!" Alejandro and Maria said, throwing their arms around his waist.

Paco hugged them tightly, then looked at Miguel. "You can't speak to your big bro?"

Miguel didn't move, but he nodded and said, "What's up?" I know Miguel had issues because he loved Paco something fierce and he'd shared with me how he had nightmares of Paco being killed in the streets.

Paco was about to say something to Miguel when a police cruiser turned onto the street. If ever I'd had any doubt that my son was still into illicit activities, the way his whole body tensed left little doubt.

"Are you okay, *mijo*?" I asked.

His eyes stayed on the cruiser. I couldn't be sure, but it seemed as if my son was positioning himself in case he had to take off running.

Not until the cruiser had passed us did Paco relax and answer me.

"Yeah, yeah. I'm straight," he said. He stood erect, and I could tell he was forcing himself to act casual. "Where y'all headed?"

"To the zoo!" Alejandro announced.

"You should come," Maria added.

208

"Nah, I . . . I just came to see you guys."

"Paco, what's going on?" I couldn't help but ask. He was so nervous. Though his hands were in his pockets, he was shaking. "Are you in some kind of trouble?"

"Come on, Ma, don't start," he said. "I . . . I was just around and wanted to come by and see you guys. But if y'all are headed out . . ." He shrugged.

All three of my other children looked at me as if they wanted me to do something.

"Well, maybe we could wait on going to the z—"

"No!" Alejandro said before I could finish my sentence.

"Nah, go on," Paco said. "I can, umm, I —" He shifted nervously. My maternal instinct told me my child was indeed in trouble. But I knew after our blowup last time, I needed to tread lightly.

"You know what, *mijo?* The kids have been waiting all week for this trip to the zoo. So, I don't want to disappoint them, but why don't you go on inside and warm yourself up something to eat? There are some leftover tacos from yesterday, or you can find something else to eat. Then you can just take a nap, or relax until we get back." I couldn't help it, I touched his cheek. "I'd love to cook your favorite dinner when I get back."

"Enchiladas?" he asked, his eyes wide with childhood innocence.

"Yes, extra spicy."

His hand went to his stomach. "Okay, b-but only if you're okay with it."

"It would make me very happy."

I didn't know what trouble my son was running from. My first instinct had been drugs. But my maternal instincts told me it wasn't that. It was fear that had my son on the run. And if I could keep Paco at the apartment, I'd know he was safe for now.

"A'ight," he replied.

I smiled as relief swept through my body. If only I could get him to stay for good.

"Come on," I said, as I walked back up the steps to our home. I unlocked the door and let Paco in. I fought the urge to tell him not to do anything bad, and just smiled.

"Make yourself at home. It is your home. And we'll be back soon." Without thinking I leaned over and kissed my son on the head.

He reached his arms around me and squeezed me tight. I couldn't remember the last time he'd done that. Something was wrong. Paco was good at heart. But the gang had hardened him. I knew he'd found his way into some serious trouble.

"Thank you, Ma," he said.

I flashed a warm smile, once again fighting the urge to push. "That's what I'm here for. That's what I'll always be here for," I told him.

I silently thanked God for sending my son home, as I closed the door and headed out to take my other three children to the zoo.

CHAPTER 27

Only my children could make riding a Metro bus fun. I'd pushed aside worry about Paco, rested in the gratitude that my oldest was home, then joined my children in their joy.

We'd sung as we walked to the bus stop, laughed as we transferred to the second bus that took me to work, and danced as we made our way up to the Markham Hotel.

I really should have moved closer to my job, but Miguel attended Yes Prep Southwest, a charter school where the administration didn't ask questions and just believed in educating young minds. Since I wasn't in the business of giving answers, the school was perfect. I didn't want to risk the public system, and besides, my son was thriving there.

"Come on, children," I said once we reached the revolving doors that led into the hotel lobby.

"How long before we get to the zoo?" Alejandro whined.

"Sweetie, I told you we're going to go pick up my paycheck. I'll go cash it, and then we'll have lunch before we go to the zoo."

"Okay," he said, dejected.

"Just have patience, sweetheart," I reminded him. "We're going to have a fantastic day." I tousled his curly black hair, then made my way inside the hotel where I'd been working for the last six years. It wasn't the best of jobs, but the pay was decent. I liked the people that I worked with, and the woman who had referred me for the job, Rosa, was one of my closest friends.

"Hey, Wayne," I said to the front desk clerk, who always greeted me with a smile.

"Good morning, pretty lady," he said. "I thought you were off today."

"I am."

Then he snapped his fingers. "Oh yeah, it's payday."

"It must be nice to forget that," I laughed.

"No, I'm just in the modern age. I have direct deposit. I don't know why you don't set it up."

"One day," I replied. I didn't do direct deposits because I didn't do banks. As long as Herman at the corner store cashed my check, I was perfectly fine.

213

"Is Lois in the back?" I said, asking about our human resources director.

He nodded. "She is."

"Thanks."

I turned to my children. "Kids, have a seat over there." I pointed to the chairs by the entrance. "Mommy will be right back and then we'll have a fantastic day."

Alejandro was about to protest, but thankfully Miguel stepped up. "Come on, bubba," Miguel said, taking his hand. "Let's play I Spy until Mom comes back."

"I love you guys," I said, blowing them kisses.

"We love you, too, Mom," Maria said, catching my kiss and putting it over her heart — one of our favorite games. "Now, hurry."

"Of course!" I darted across the lobby and toward the back offices. I had just rounded the corner when I bumped into my supervisor, Sergio.

"Oh, my God, Anna," he said. "I am so glad to see you."

"Hello, Sergio. How are you doing today?" I said. My over-the-top French boss was so extra, but I liked him a lot.

"Horrible!" he screamed. "Mary Louise just threw up all over the second floor because she has some kind of virus, and Valencia called out. I need you to work."

My eyes bucked. Normally, I would've never turned down work, but I just couldn't today.

"Oh, I'm so sorry. I can't. I just came to pick up my check. I have my kids and we're going to the zoo and spending the rest of the day together."

He grasped both of my hands. "Anna, I am desperate," he said. "I have a big conference coming to check in in a couple of hours."

"No, no, no," I muttered, shaking my head and suddenly wishing I had direct deposit.

"Please?" he said. Then, before I could respond, he continued, "When you needed to take time off the books to deal with Paco, who was there? Who took care of you with Corporate? Who lets you leave without being docked every time one of your kids is sick?"

I bit my bottom lip, fighting off curse words at the carrot that he'd just dangled. "Please don't do this to me, Sergio."

"Anna, I'm just asking for an hour. Please? You work fast, so that's all it will take. Rosa is the only one here. And there is no way she can get all these rooms done on time. We had a full house last night. I'm cleaning rooms," he said, motioning to a cart behind him. "And you know I haven't cleaned rooms in five years."

I nodded. That was the truth. Since they made Sergio a supervisor, he was excellent at supervising. And that was it.

"I am desperate, Anna," he said.

I sighed and he seized the moment.

"Just do your normal. The rooms on the third floor. We've already knocked out the first two floors, and cleaned up that disgusting mess from Mary Louise. If you could do the third and fourth floors, that would be great."

"Sergio . . ."

"You can be out of here in an hour — two, tops. I promise I'll make it up to you. I'll give you that time off for the state fair."

I groaned. Sergio knew how badly I had wanted to go to the state fair in Dallas. One of my church members had given the kids and me tickets to the fair and vouchers for food and rides. Since we never got to go anywhere, I thought it would be a great outing for us as a family. But two other people had requested that day off before I did.

"Ugh," I groaned. "Okay, fine. Let me go tell my kids."

"You are a lifesaver," he said, kissing me on the cheek and darting off down the hall.

I took a deep breath, then walked back

into the lobby. My kids jumped up when they saw me.

"Time to go to the zoo," Alejandro sang.

The look on my face wiped the excited expression off theirs.

"Uh, Mom, what's up?" Miguel asked.

I sighed. "Kids, Mommy has to work."

"What?" all three of them said in unison.

"Not long," I quickly interjected. "Just a couple of hours."

"Mommy . . ." Alejandro whined.

"Please?" I said. "Just be patient. Here," I said, reaching into my purse, which was wrapped around my body, and pulling out a twenty-dollar bill. "Miguel, take them across the street to get some ice cream."

"Ice cream in the morning?" Miguel said.

"Yes. Is that okay with you?" I smiled, hoping it would ease their frustration.

"It's great," he said, welcoming the consolation prize. I was a stickler on how they ate, so the fact that I was encouraging ice cream before noon was a rare occurrence.

"Good. I love you all." I took all three of them by the hand and kissed them each on the cheek. "We're going to have a great time today. Just give me a little bit. I need to help out around here. Get the ice cream and then come right back and sit here in the lobby and eat it."

Thankfully, the thought of ice cream for breakfast had soothed them, and they bounced out.

I went into the back, where I stored my things in my locker, put on the extra cleaning uniform I kept on hand, grabbed a cart, and made my way up to the third floor.

Rosa was already at work. "Anna, what are you doing here?" she said when she spotted me. "I thought you were off today and taking the kids out somewhere."

"I thought so, too," I said, removing my cleaning supplies from the cart. "Sergio sucked me in because he said Valencia called out."

I didn't even like Valencia. Or rather, she didn't like me. She claimed that I'd gotten her suspended because she was smoking on the job and I'd refused to cover for her. So ever since that incident last month, she couldn't stand me.

But I told myself this was about helping Sergio, not Valencia.

"Chica, it has been an absolute nightmare around here. It seems like the whole third floor had a wild party last night."

"Mierda!"

Rosa laughed. "Wow, Sergio has you cursing." She shook her head. "Let's just knock it out so you can get back to your babies.

I've already done the rooms on this side. You can take your usual," she said, pointing to the even rooms on the other side of the hall.

I immediately went about my usual routine, scrubbing and cleaning. Rosa was right, these rooms were unusually dirty. I saw why Sergio was freaking out. After I finished 320 and 318, I headed to Room 316. This seemed to be the only room in halfway decent order. I changed the sheets on the bed, then ran the vacuum. That's when I saw an old tattered book on the floor next to the desk chair. I picked it up. This was that book that lady from the news station had asked me about. I flipped it open and started reading.

My eyes scanned some of my favorite passages.

"He shall direct thy paths," I read, stopping on one in particular because it took me back to my days in Hidalgo.

I shivered as I recalled the small pink Bible my mother placed in my hands the night Julio and I left.

"Child, stop your crying," my mother whispered. She used her hand to wipe away my tears.

"But why can't you and Daddy come with us?" I cried.

"Because we are too old to make this journey. Plus, your brother is in critical condition."

Just thinking of my brother, gunned down by the drug cartel for God only knows what, I knew why we were leaving. We had to go before they claimed someone else we loved.

"You must go with your husband and child now," my mother continued.

I'd been excited the whole time Julio had been planning our escape to America. He knew someone who knew someone, who arranged everything. Call me young and naive, but it never dawned on me that my parents weren't coming, too.

"But —"

"No buts," she said, cutting me off. "You are a woman now. A mother. And your family must always come first. You must go with your husband in search of a better life."

I looked back over my shoulder at Julio, who was waiting in the back of the room, a backpack with all of our belongings swung across his shoulder. He was so patient. I imagined I looked like a blubbering idiot.

"Take this," my mother said, pressing the Bible into my hand. "This shall be your roadmap to guide you on your journey."

I wondered how in the world a Bible was

supposed to guide me. As if she read my mind, my mother said, "If you're scared, this will help. If your faith wavers, this will help. Just keep it close and know that He will make your paths straight."

I nodded as I held the Bible close. "When will I see you and Papa again?" I asked.

She put her hand to my face. "Soon. After you create this wonderful new life, we'll come and visit."

Of course, I never saw my parents again.

And my path had yet to be made straight.

As a faithful woman, I knew God was capable of anything, but that was one area where I didn't see Him working His magic.

CHAPTER 28

I had long ago given up dreams of doing things the right way, of following the rules to gain citizenship. It was too risky. What if they denied me? What would happen to my children? I'd adopted the philosophy of it's better to ask for forgiveness than permission, and settled into my familiar existence. That was where I'd be until I left this earth. Though I didn't regularly attend church now because I worked on Sundays, my Catholic upbringing was deep-rooted — but I'll admit, when I looked at my struggles, sometimes it was hard to remain faithful.

Julio would spend his evenings reading from our Bible, verses about faith. He always believed that one day we would be legitimate U.S. citizens. I didn't see how that would ever happen, but I was glad my husband had been faithful until the day he died. It had given him something to hold on to.

"Hey. My vacuum isn't picking up good," Rosa said, sticking her head into the room and interrupting my thoughts. "Let me see yours really quick. What's that?" she asked, looking over my shoulder at the book that I'd just set down.

"It's a Bible," I said, turning it to face her.

"Ewww, that thing looks like it's five hundred years old. Did somebody leave it here?"

"Yeah, the other day when I was cleaning up, one of the people that was staying in this room asked me about it."

"Oh. Take it to Lost and Found," Rose said as she wrapped the cord up from my vacuum. "Though I doubt anyone would be coming in search of that."

"I'll take it to Lost and Found on my way out. Right now I just need to hurry and finish because my kids are downstairs waiting."

"Okay. I'll go do my rooms, then I'll bring the vacuum back."

"I told Sergio I'd do two floors, so after I finish here, I'll do the fourth-floor even rooms, then I've got to go."

"Lucky you. Have fun with the babies today," she said.

"I'm looking forward to it."

Rosa headed toward the door. "Kiss them

for . . ." Her words trailed off, and I turned to see what had made her stop talking mid-sentence. Standing in the door were Sergio and five official-looking men.

"Hi, Mr. Baptiste," Rosa said. "I . . . I was just coming to use Anna's vacuum."

He didn't say a word to her as she hurried around him.

"I'm almost done on this floor," I said, looking at Sergio and trying to decipher the nervous expression on his face. My eyes darted between him and the group of men, all of whom wore navy-blue windbreakers. And then I saw the words written on their jackets and my heart sank. ICE. Immigration and Customs Enforcement.

"Uh, Anna, I'm sorry, but you need to come with us," Sergio said. He spoke in his supervisor tone, and that, in and of itself, frightened me.

"Why? What's going on?" My eyes continued doing that dance between them all. "I mean, I'm almost finished, but I have work to do if I'm going to complete the rooms in time for the conference. People will need to check in," I said, moving to finish making the bed. I guess I was thinking if I could just get back to work, I could make the sight before me go away.

"Ma'am. That wasn't a request." The ICE

agent who spoke stepped around Sergio. His fiery red hair made him look like the devil.

The devil had come to destroy my life.

"Are you Anna Rodríguez?" he asked.

I contemplated feigning ignorance, breaking out in Spanish and pretending I couldn't understand English. But since I'd already opened my big mouth . . .

"Yes, I-I'm Anna," I said, stammering my words out.

The devil reached down, took my arms, and put them behind my back, turning me around in the process. "Anna Rodríguez, you are under arrest for illegal entry into the United States, illegal use of a Social Security number, and felony criminal impersonation. Anything you say can be used against you in subsequent proceedings. You have the right to an attorney at no cost to the government."

"What? What's going on?" I asked. My panicked eyes turned to Sergio. "Mr. Baptiste?"

"I'm so sorry," Sergio said. "I-I had no idea. They just showed up here . . . claimed an anonymous call tipped them off . . . I didn't know . . ."

An anonymous tip. Valencia had called in sick. She had to know they'd call me in. She'd made a comment a year ago, inquiring if I was undocumented. When I didn't answer, I could tell she was suspicious. Was this her payback for me not covering for her smoking on the job?

"Sergio, no, no. Why is this happening?" I cried.

Another one of the ICE agents, this one a gray-haired, spotty-faced man, said, "Get her out, guys."

"Must you do that?" Sergio said, his voice filled with panic. "We have guests."

I didn't know if he was more concerned about my well-being or how this looked for the hotel. It didn't matter. I just needed to convince him not to let me go.

"Sergio, tell them I'm a good worker. Please tell them they don't need to do this!"

"Sir," Sergio said toward the devil. "She's no threat! Please. Just allow her to walk with you without the handcuffs."

None of the ICE agents said a word as they led me out of the room, ignoring both Sergio's and my pleas.

I was mortified. I had worked here for so long and lived in fear of this day. "No, no. Please don't do this," I cried.

But they weren't moved by my words. They pushed me out of the door, toward the elevator. Tears started streaming down my face.

"My children," I said. "My children are downstairs."

Rosa came running down the hall just as the elevator doors opened. "Anna, what's going on?"

"Rosa, get my kids," I cried as the man pushed me into the elevator. They all ignored my pleas. I only stopped when the elevator doors opened downstairs and I saw my children staring right at me.

Miguel was the first to spot me. "Mama!" he yelled, jumping up and running toward me.

Alejandro and Maria noticed and followed. The two of them immediately threw their arms around my waist as Miguel shouted, "Mama, what's happening? Why do they have you in handcuffs? Are you going to jail?"

"Nooooo," Alejandro cried.

"Mommy, what's happening?" Maria said.

With each outburst my heart broke a little more. Their tears made mine flow harder.

"Get the kids out of the way," the devil ICE agent said.

Sergio and Rosa, who had bolted from the stairwell, tried to pull my kids away.

"It's okay," I said to them. "Mommy is okay. Just go with Miss Rosa."

The officer snatched my arm to lead me away.

"Can I comfort my kids?" I yelled.

My raised voice frightened my kids even more because Alejandro started panting, the first sign of the asthma attacks that regularly plagued him.

I leaned closer, adjusting my arms behind my back so they didn't see my discomfort. I tried to push back my fear as I said, "Mommy needs you guys to go with Miss Rosa and listen to her until I come back, okay?" I looked directly at Alejandro. "And I need you to stay calm so your asthma doesn't flare up. Can you do that for Mommy?"

His chest heaved, but slowed just a bit as he nodded.

"Why are they taking you to jail?" Miguel asked.

The ICE agent lost patience. He grabbed me and all but dragged me out. As Rosa and Sergio fought to contain my crying kids, as patrons in the lobby stared in horror, they dragged me out like I was a wanted murderer.

I knew this day would haunt my nightmares for the rest of my life.

CHAPTER 29

This had been my nightmare for decades. The spotlight that had made me live in the shadows since I set foot on American soil. The fear of deportation had hung over me for nineteen years. I'd even skipped the photo shoot when I'd made employee of the year for the Markham because I didn't want my picture and name to go on their corporate website. I didn't want anything that would draw attention to me. All I wanted was a better life for my children. Was that too much to ask?

I had a frightening thought. What if they deported me without letting me see my kids? What if they shipped me back to Hidalgo without even letting me say goodbye? The thought turned my stomach upside down and brought fresh tears to my eyes.

I pulled my sweater tightly around me, a shiver sifting through me even though the room had to be at least eighty degrees.

I didn't know where I was, but it looked like some kind of holding center. I assumed for immigration since everyone in here was like me, Latino and terrified. I had been here at least six hours, and they'd been the longest six hours of my life.

"You okay?" a lady asked as she sat down next to me. I'd noticed her earlier. She was the only one here who didn't look scared. Maybe it was the tattoos across her neck or her stringy blond hair and dark roots, but she looked like this place was her second home.

"I said, are you okay?" she repeated.

I didn't answer, just shook my head.

"This must be your first time," she said.

I nodded.

"Yeah, you looking all clean-cut, like J.Lo. It's my third time," she casually said, "so I know they will personally take me and drop me on the other side of the border." She laughed. "As if that's gonna stop me. I'll risk coming back again and again rather than going back to what I came from."

Now my stomach wasn't just in knots. I felt like I was actually going to be sick.

The woman continued. "Have you had your one call?"

"I get a call?"

"Don't you watch *Law & Order*?" she said.

"No. I don't watch much TV. But I thought, I mean, since I'm not a U.S. citizen . . ."

"You thought what? That they would treat us like crap?" She shrugged. "They do, but that's the beauty of America. We still have some rights. You get a free call, so make sure you ask for it."

She leaned back and closed her eyes, signaling that this conversation was over. I couldn't believe how calm she was. But I was grateful for her knowledge of the system.

I stood and gripped the bars as I called out to one of the ICE officers.

"Excuse me, I've been here a long time. May I please have my one call?"

The female agent first flashed a look of indifference at me. I don't know if she saw the terror in my eyes, but she came over and opened the gate.

"Come on," she said.

"Thank you," I replied. Immediately, others started yelling and pleading. But she ignored them and quickly locked the gate.

She directed me toward a phone hanging on a back wall. I picked up the handset and gave the operator who came on Rosa's home number, grateful that it was one of the few I knew by heart.

"Rosa," I said as soon as she accepted the collect call. "Thank God you answered."

"Oh, Anna. How are you?"

"Not good," I said, struggling not to cry. "I don't have much time. Are my babies okay?"

"Yes, they're scared, but they're okay."

"What about Alejandro's asthma?" I asked.

"It's under control. Thank God for Miguel. He got him calmed down and taken care of."

That gave me a small sense of relief.

"Tell them I love them."

"They know that," she replied. "So what's going on? Where are you?"

I glanced around the room. With the dirty brown walls, steel tables, and raggedy wooden desks, it looked like an old school that had been renovated to house criminals. My God, I was a criminal.

I noticed a sign on the wall and rattled the information off for Rosa. "It says I'm at the Smith Detention Center."

"I know where that is," she replied.

"Do you think you can come see me?"

"Of course. I will come as soon as I can."

Back in the cell, I mumbled the Lord's Prayer until I dozed off. I was awakened by the sound of someone shouting my name.

"Anna Rodríguez?" an officer called out.

"Yes, yes." I jumped up. I don't know why, but I was praying that some miracle had happened and they were telling me I was going home. Unfortunately, all the deputy said was, "Someone is here to see you."

I sighed as I made my way to the door. As I waited for the bars to open, I looked back over my shoulder and desperately wished that I would never see these people again.

The third-timer had told me that from here, we would go before an immigration judge who would decide our fate. I was dreading the thought of being sent back to my native land.

My children were American citizens, but what did that mean if I wasn't here with them? They couldn't stay because no one could take care of them. Paco wouldn't go back, so I would be forced to leave him alone and take my children back to a country where they didn't know the language, didn't know a soul, and would be subjected to a life of destitution and crime.

"Oh, my God," Rosa said as I slid into the seat across from her. "Are you okay?"

I was grateful that Rosa was legal — she'd gotten her papers nine years ago. Otherwise I probably would've been unable to see her.

"No, I'm not all right," I cried. "This place . . . it's just so horrible."

"What happened?" she said.

I took a deep breath. Rosa had no idea I wasn't legal. She had no idea about the illegal Social Security number that I'd been using for years because no one knew outside of Julio. He'd just come home with the cards one day — announced we were unofficially official and I didn't ask any questions. We'd gone out to celebrate that night and had been working ever since.

"I . . . I'm not supposed to be working in the U.S."

"What do you mean? You told me you had papers when you asked for this job," she said, confused.

I looked down, ashamed of the lie I had told my friend. "I do have papers, but they don't belong to me."

Her hand went to her mouth. "Oh, my God. You were working under a fake Social Security number?" she said.

I could only nod. "I was desperate. I never meant to deceive you, I just . . ."

She leaned forward and immediately shhh'd me. "Okay, we're not going to have this conversation here." She lowered her voice. "You never know who could be recording."

"I don't think it matters anymore," I said. "They obviously know. That's why I'm here. Did Sergio set me up?" I asked.

"No. I don't think so," Rosa replied. "He was absolutely dumbfounded and he kept talking about losing his best worker, and then he threatened the rest of us that we all better be on the up-and-up because of how this was going to reflect on the hotel. Rumor is that Valencia called INS."

So my guess was probably true. I sighed, then dabbed at my eyes.

"I'm so sorry," I said. "I didn't mean to make things so difficult for you." My heart sank at the thought that no matter what happened, my job was as good as gone.

"What are you going to do?" she asked.

"I don't know." I would definitely have to figure out my job situation. But right now, my focus was on something more important. "Be honest. How are my children?"

She hesitated, like she wasn't sure how much she should tell me. Finally, she said, "Not good. Alejandro won't stop crying. Miguel is in a state of shock. The good news is that Paco was still at your house so he knows what is going on. He's with the children now."

"Thank you so much." Paco gave me grief, but he loved his siblings. I could take comfort in knowing that he and Rosa would make sure they were taken care of. Plus, the kids always enjoyed being around Rosa's two children. "Please tell them all that I love them. And . . . and I'll be home soon." Even as the words left my mouth, they felt like a lie.

"Will you?" she asked. Her eyes told me she already knew the answer to that.

"I honestly don't know," I said, a tear trickling down my face.

"Be strong, *mi hija,*" she said. "We'll figure something out. My neighbor's cousin went through this. She said you need to get an attorney right away." She sighed. "The problem is, I don't have any money for an attorney. And I know you don't, either."

"I don't."

"Do we know anyone that can help?" she said. "My neighbor is trying to raise awareness about her cousin's case. She's doing a lot of stuff on social media. She's even been trying to maybe get the case on the news."

The news.

"That's it," I said, recalling the lady in Room 316. My hand went to my apron.

"What are you doing?" Rosa asked.

I frantically dug down in my apron pocket and pulled out the business card.

"What's that?" Rosa asked.

236

"The lady. The lady that was staying in the room. She gave me her card. She is one of those TV newspeople."

"What are you talking about?"

"Savannah Graham," I said, reading the card before turning it to face Rosa. "She's a reporter for Channel 26. She was staying in the room the other day when I went to clean it. She was super nice to me. Maybe . . ." I was too scared to even think of the possibilities.

"Oh, wow. You think she could help?" Rosa asked.

"I don't know but maybe she knows an attorney who can help me."

"Well, I say it's worth a try. You have nothing to lose and everything to gain."

"Here." I slid Rosa the card. "Call her, please. Tell her I'm the housekeeper from the hotel. Explain my situation. Let her know I'm law-abiding, remind her about my kids. Tell her everything. She was nice. Maybe she can help."

Rosa took the card. "I'll call her the minute I step out."

For the first time since I had arrived at the detention center, I felt a glimmer of hope.

CHAPTER 30

Rosa had delivered.

I couldn't believe that Savannah Graham was sitting across from me, ready to hear my story.

I don't know what kind of strings Rosa had pulled, but Savannah was here in her official capacity not twenty-four hours after we'd come up with the idea to call her.

"How are you?" she asked, once she was settled across from me.

I shrugged. "No use lying. Horrible," I replied. "I just want to get home to my kids."

"That's understandable," she said, giving me a warm smile.

"You look . . ." I finally smiled as I took in her appearance, "happy."

This professional woman in her tailored suit, with her hair perfectly curled and makeup flawless, was a far cry from the disheveled woman who I met in Room 316.

Savannah was pensive for a moment, then said, "I wouldn't say that I'm happy. But I'm healing. I think that's the word for it. Healing and on my way to happy. Thanks to your wisdom, I sat still and listened." The gratitude in her eyes was sincere.

"Good," I said. "I know I can be a chatterbox, but when I feel led to talk to people, I can't help but speak up."

"Well, I'm glad you did. And now it's my turn to return the favor. You may not know it, but I do a lot of immigration stories at the station. So I'm well versed on the subject. What I would like to do is get your story out to the public. Having public support can help bolster your case."

"I want whatever you think will help," I said. "I can't thank you enough for coming. I don't know if this can help, but if there's a chance . . ."

My words trailed off as a wild-haired blonde entered the room. She wore a gray, baggy sweater, white tee, and jeans that looked two sizes too big.

"Oh, this is Jerri Tapper," Savannah said as the woman entered. "She is with the Freedom Coalition, an immigration rights organization. I hope you don't mind that I asked her to sit in with us."

I nodded. "That's fine." If they could help

me, I would gladly have her and anyone else sit in. I no longer cared about being private. If I needed an army to get me home to my kids, then bring on the troops.

"Hello," Jerri said, leaning in and shaking my hand.

"Hi." I turned to Savannah as Jerri took a seat in the corner; then I took a deep breath and told myself I didn't have time to beat around the bush. "Am I going to be deported?" I asked.

"I don't know much about your case yet, but not if we can help it," Savannah said. "First things first, are your children okay?"

The fact that she had asked about my children warmed my heart and let me know I was doing the right thing by talking with her.

"As well as can be expected," I replied. "I mean, I guess they are. I haven't seen them and I know they're terrified, but they're with my friend Rosa, the one who called you. I know she's taking good care of them."

Savannah continued, "Well, we're going to do everything we can to help. We've gotten clearance to film because we think that's the best way to get your story out. It will air tomorrow on the nine o'clock news. Are you okay with that?"

Instinct made me tense up. Anytime I'd

seen a camera over the last two decades, I'd gone in the opposite direction. But now I knew that to have any type of chance, this was my only option.

"Yes, it's fine."

She looked back at her cameraman. "Rodney, are you ready?"

"Gimme a minute," he said, fumbling with one of the lights.

Rodney continued setting up his equipment and tripod as Savannah turned back to me and made small talk.

"I'm ready," he finally said.

Savannah flashed a reassuring smile. "I want you to relax and talk directly to me. Pretend the camera isn't there."

I patted down my hair, thinking about what a mess I must look, but she stopped me. "No, we want you to be yourself."

"I'm rolling," Rodney said.

"Let's start," Savannah began, her tone turning professional. "Anna, tell us, how did you arrive in the United States, and why are you in this situation?"

I tried to keep my composure as I traveled back to one of the most terrifying times in my life.

"I came when I was just eighteen," I began. "I've been here ever since. My husband — God rest his soul — and I just wanted a better life than what existed in our home of Hidalgo, Mexico. Unfortunately, the only way I could work was by obtaining a false Social Security number." I didn't bother to hide the shame I felt about breaking the law. I simply wanted to lay everything on the table. "But I'm a good citizen. I pay taxes. I'm not a threat. But now they're about to tear me away from my family."

"Tell me about the journey here," Savannah said.

Another deep sigh as I dug up that awful memory. "It was about thirty-five of us. We paid this guy fifteen thousand dollars. Julio and I had saved some money. His father was in agriculture, and when he died, he left a little money and that's how we got the rest. A gringo got us across the border, and then we were in a truck for what seemed like days. It was hot, and two of the people didn't make it." I bit my bottom lip. For years I'd blocked the memory of that journey out of my mind. One of the people who didn't survive was the only person I knew, a childhood friend named Autoro. Watching him die had been one of the worst ordeals I had ever endured. "Paco had just been born, and Julio said there was no way we'd let him grow up in crime-ravaged Hidalgo.

We both had lost countless relatives to the drug cartel and the violence of the area. We were determined to come to America to give our children a better life. The journey was the worst experience of our lives. But we had heard the stories of this being the land of prosperity, and anything was better than where we were."

She scribbled on a notepad and turned the page as the cameraman continued filming.

When I was done, I felt like I had purged years' worth of secrets, since I had never talked about my journey to America.

"I know I was wrong. But I had tried to come to America the right way. I finished school early. I tried to get a student visa, but I was denied. There was no work in Hidalgo. There was no opportunity. That was our driving force."

"And you were eighteen at the time?"

I nodded.

"And you're how old now?"

"Thirty-seven."

"Wow. So, you've been here for nineteen years?"

"Yes," I answered. "All I have tried to do is be a law-abiding citizen. I pay my taxes with the Social Security number because I didn't want to feel like I was cheating the government. I've never had government benefits. I volunteer at my church."

"So, you're the ideal candidate when we talk about welcoming people into our country," Savannah said.

"One would think so, but it seems all that matters is that I came in the wrong way." My voice cracked at the harsh reality.

She scribbled some more. "If you don't mind" — she pointed to Rodney, who had picked his camera up with the tripod and moved behind us — "our photographer is going to get a couple of shots from other angles."

I nodded again and continued talking. Savannah spent another ten minutes talking to me and finally ended with, "Anna, what do you want?"

I thought long and hard about that question. And the answer was the same as it had always been.

"I want to come out of the shadows. I want my own Social Security number. I want to be an American citizen. But now" — I lowered my head — "I don't think that will ever be possible." I swallowed the lump that built in my throat whenever I thought about this. "At least my children are American citizens, but my two youngest are seven and nine. The idea of being separated from them tears at my soul. But I'd do it. I'd give them up so that they can enjoy life in America," I said with conviction.

A slight mist covered both Savannah's and Jerri's eyes. "Well, we're going to do what we can," Savannah said with a catch in her voice. "I hate to have to ask you this," she added, "but do you think we could talk with your children? That would add a whole element to personalizing your story."

"Yes, that will be fine," I said. "You can call Rosa and she'll arrange things."

"Great, we'll do that as soon as we leave. I still have Rosa's number."

"Thank you," I told her, squeezing her hand. "You have no idea how much this means."

As the cameraman began wrapping up his equipment, Jerri moved closer to me.

"Mrs. Rodríguez," she said, "I am here today because at the Freedom Coalition, we are committed to helping immigration cases like yours." She smiled. "We firmly live by the creed: when a foreigner resides in your land, do not mistreat them."

I returned her smile. "One of my favorites."

"With your blessing, I want to make several legislators and elected officials aware of your situation. Nothing would give me greater joy than to make yours one of our success stories. Nothing would give me greater joy than to set your path straight."

He will make your paths straight.

I hugged her as my answer.

CHAPTER 31

I was a faithful woman, but right about now that faith was truly being tested. Forty-eight hours had passed and I was still in jail, or a detention center, or whatever you called this place. I didn't care what the name was. All I knew was that I wasn't at home. I knew my children had to be losing their minds. Thank God for Paco because despite all the grief that he had given me over the past few years, Alejandro, Maria, and Miguel loved him something crazy. So I was sure he was keeping them entertained and, hopefully, keeping their minds off my absence. Though that gave me some comfort, I was still ready to get out of here. Last night a fight had broken out between two women over a blanket, and after the officers separated them, I'd been unable to go back to sleep.

Because I was so tired, I'd been dozing off and on. In fact, I had just dozed off when I heard someone yell, "Hey, isn't that her?"

My eyes opened to see several people staring at me, and then at the screen.

"Hey, J.Lo, you're on TV," the three-timer said to me.

We all jumped up, including me, and raced to the bars and peered through to the forty-two-inch screen mounted on the wall of the ICE office.

All of the officers were tuned to the TV, where Savannah Graham had just finished saying something.

"Turn it up," somebody from the cell yelled.

"Sit down and shut up," one of the guards replied.

"Come on, man," the three-timer said. "That's her." She pointed at me. "Let her see herself."

The female officer who had let me use the phone walked over, picked up the remote, and turned the volume up.

". . . And so, Anna Rodríguez said all she wants is to build a better life than the one she was born into," Savannah said.

Then my face popped up on the screen again, and I couldn't hear what words I said because the people in the cell started yelling.

"Shut up so we can hear the TV," someone standing next to me said.

They quieted down as my interview continued. This all seemed surreal for me, a person that had never wanted any type of attention. I had now been thrust stage front and center.

My interview concluded and Savannah wrapped up her report with "The Freedom Coalition plans to picket this evening and are working to get Rodríguez released on her own recognizance."

"How'd you get so lucky?" someone yelled from behind me.

I couldn't answer that. I didn't know what I'd done. Other than try to stay faithful in even the darkest hour.

"Shoot, we're all here illegally," someone else said. "Where is our story?"

The three-timer turned to the people throwing out questions. "Everybody ain't meant to take a divine path. Some of you are worthless and need to be sent home. So lay off her and let her get her blessings."

"Ummm, isn't she a career criminal?" someone muttered from the back.

"What did you say?" the three-timer muttered as she stomped over to the person who'd said it.

I blocked them out of my mind as I clutched the necklace bearing my children's names. I thought about the divine being that had laid this all out so perfectly. My only hope was that it would make a difference. My report wrapped up and the guards put the TV back on mute and everyone slowly went back to their respective spots.

The cornucopia of thoughts had kept me tossing and turning all night. I couldn't help but wonder what, if anything, would come of the interview.

That's where my mind was when an officer approached the cell just after they'd given us our breakfast of dry toast and lumpy oatmeal.

"Anna Rodríguez?" he said.

I jumped up, wiping the sleep from my eyes. "Yes, that's me."

"Your attorney is here."

"My attorney?"

He didn't reply as he opened the cell to let me out. I followed behind him to the attorney-client room, where inside I saw Jerri from the Freedom Coalition and a distinguished-looking balding man. He smiled as he saw me.

"Hello, Mrs. Rodríguez." He extended his hand.

"Hi," I replied, shaking his hand but looking at Jerri for answers.

"My name is Oliver Johnson, and I am an

attorney with the law firm of Johnson, McHarden, and Olympia."

Jerri was grinning behind him, but I was still clueless. On the list of things I'd hoped for, I hadn't even thought about an attorney. "I know this is all overwhelming because things are moving pretty fast, but Oliver saw the story and immediately contacted me," she said.

I waited for her to continue.

Oliver snapped open his briefcase as he picked up the conversation. "I am very excited because you are the perfect candidate that we've been looking for to represent in a groundbreaking immigration case. Our firm is a leader in immigration law. With the recent deportation enforcements, we've been looking for a case to highlight our struggle, and we think yours is perfect."

I was speechless.

"Please, have a seat," he said, motioning to the chair on the other side of the table.

Jerri couldn't stop grinning, which to me was a good sign. Oliver removed a piece of paper from his briefcase and slid it across the table to me.

"I have already filed a motion to have you released, and it will go before the judge in the morning," he said.

"In the morning?" I said. "So, you mean I

could go home tomorrow?"

Jerri nodded. "That's exactly what he means."

I couldn't help but smile as my heart danced with relief. "Oh, that is so wonderful. But what happens after that?" I said.

"Well, it will be a long journey, but because of the president's travel ban and all of the attention to his crackdown on immigrants, we expect we'll get a lot of publicity." Oliver took out another piece of paper and passed it to me. "This is our standard agreement to represent. If you're amenable, we'll immediately move forward to have the charges against you vacated."

"But . . . but I broke the law," I said.

"And you will probably have to pay a price for that, but because you have been here so long, because your children are American citizens — and in the past, the court has been sympathetic to parents of American citizens — our hope is that we can convince the judge to give you some type of probation. Have you check in with an immigration officer and then —"

Jerri cut him off. It was obvious that she could no longer contain her excitement. "Let me tell her." She smiled at me. "And then begin your path to citizenship."

I was floored. "You mean, I could really

become a citizen?"

"I can't make any promises," Oliver said. "But that's our goal. It's a lengthy and extensive process, but if there's ever been a candidate that America should welcome into its ranks, it's a person like you."

I couldn't help it. I stood and threw my arms around Oliver. The move must have caught him off guard, because he said, "Wow. Okay. Well, that's what I like. I always like to be paid in hugs."

That made me stop, and I stepped back. "Oh, my God. I can't afford you," I said as if that problem had just dawned on me.

Jerri spoke up before he could. "That is the least of your concerns," she said. "The Freedom Coalition has that part all taken care of."

"But —"

"But nothing," she replied. "Now, if you are looking for some way to return the favor, we have an opening in our main office for an assistant. It's full-time, not a whole lot of money, but probably more than you made at the Markham. And if you don't have office skills, I can train you. So, what do you think?"

I stared at her in disbelief. "I think, yes. Absolutely, yes!"

She smiled and hugged me again. "Now,

you just give Oliver here everything he needs, and we'll make sure he is properly compensated."

"This is a calling for us," Oliver said. "We work with Jerri and the organization. We don't want you to be concerned with that."

"Thank you, Jesus," I said.

Oliver flashed a warm smile. "Yep, He was definitely looking out for you today."

CHAPTER 32

I had dozed back off with thoughts of going home when I felt someone shake me.

"Hey, Superstar, you're on TV again!" I glanced up from the hard cot at one of my cell mates, who was pointing to the TV outside the cell.

I jumped up, assuming that they were running Savannah's story again. I was praying for some kind of miraculous update. Instead, I saw the reporter for the NBC station. The volume was up loud, and when my picture popped up on the screen, the room quieted.

". . . Anna Rodríguez has been at the center of an immigration debate, with noted attorney Oliver Johnson leading the fight to keep the woman from being deported," the reporter said. "But in an exclusive Channel 2 investigation, we've learned that fight may have just intensified. That's because police say this man . . ."

My heart plummeted when an enhanced surveillance picture of my son Paco popped up on the screen.

". . . may have been involved in last month's shooting of six-year-old Lupita Garcia. You may remember she was the little girl gunned down outside of the Main Event in Stafford as she was leaving with her family. Police say two men, Paco Rodríguez and another unidentified suspect, were firing at a rival gang member. Channel 2 can exclusively report that Rodríguez is the son of Anna Rodríguez, the woman at the center of the immigration debate."

My mouth fell open in horror, and I had to hold on to the bars to steady myself.

The reporter continued. "We're told that the son is undocumented, just like his mother. And anti-immigration activists have jumped on that piece of news."

A white man with jet-black hair and a mustache that made him look like the Lone Ranger popped up on the screen.

"This is exactly what we're fighting against," he barked at the camera. The chyron under his name said he was with the Anti-Immigration Foundation. "This here gangbanger killed a little girl. We let these illegals into the country and they send us their worst. They're bringing drugs. They're bringing crime. They're rapists . . ." he continued, repeating the refrain that I'd been hearing for the past two years. "And they're murderers! The news is trying to paint that lady as a saint, but if she hadn't snuck in our country, her gangsta son wouldn't be here and that little girl would be alive today!"

The sins of the child.

Plenty of American citizens had children who did bad things beyond their control, but I was being lambasted because of a son I couldn't control.

I squeezed the bars tighter because I felt myself hyperventilating. It was then that I noticed the way the detention officers were looking at me — as if I was scum. As if I had somehow put the gun in Paco's hands. And the way the others in the cell were looking at me — as if I had messed up things for them — made my heart want to cry.

"Dang, J.Lo," the three-timer said as she walked past me. "Your boy is killing kids?" She shook her head and sat on the far side of the cell. I guessed this news had made me a leper.

A guard approached me, his disdain evident. "Is that true?"

"I . . . I . . . I . . ."

"Is that your son?" he asked when I couldn't get my answer out.

I nodded. "B-but, h-he doesn't live with me."

"Hmph" was all he said as he stormed off.

Someone muted the volume on the television, and everyone slowly returned to whatever they'd been doing. I needed to talk to Rosa and try to find out what in the world was going on. But judging from the scowl on the officers' faces, no one would be letting me use a phone anytime soon.

"So I have good news, and I have bad news."

I trembled as I sat in the small conference room with Mr. Oliver. Last night had been one of the longest of my life. A guard had felt sorry for me and allowed me to use the phone, and I'd called Rosa, who told me Paco had taken off earlier in the day. After the news report — which she said everyone in our neighborhood was talking about — she was doubtful that he would return. So my heart broke as I wondered if the report was true. Did Paco really have anything to do with that little girl's death? Then I wondered what that meant if he did. And finally, I wondered what that meant for me.

Judging by the look on Oliver's and Jerri's faces, it wasn't good news for me.

"Here's where we stand," he began. His optimistic light from the other day had definitely dimmed. "I'd love to hand you your citizenship papers and we wrap this up in a nice little bow, but unfortunately, with these new revelations it's not going to be that easy."

I trembled with nervous anticipation as he continued. "Based on the surveillance tape, the district attorney can't tell if it was your son or the other boy who fired the fatal shot. But your son is the only one who they have a clear ID on. Turns out Paco went to a convenience store about an hour before the shooting and tried to buy beer. They wouldn't sell it to him and the clerk still had it behind the counter. When he saw the surveillance tape and info about the shooting on the news, he recognized your son and told police. They were able to pull Paco's prints from the beer. Regardless of whether Paco killed the girl or not, under Texas law, he's just as guilty."

"What does that mean?" I asked as my heart plummeted into the pit of my stomach.

"It means the DA has leverage," Mr. Oliver answered. "And let me shoot straight. While they're two different entities, any kind of legal trouble can make things difficult.

You're facing a long road, but the DA said he may be able to get INS to work with them — provided you help them turn your son in."

"What?" I said, tearing up. "Turn him in?"

"I know it's hard. But it's a choice you'll have to make," Mr. Oliver said. "Are you going to sacrifice your son for your other three kids?"

I couldn't believe this was the position that I was being put in. I loved all of my kids. Was I really supposed to give up Paco in order to be there for my other children? And what if I turned Paco in and they still deported me?

Finally, I asked, "Why do they think I can get him to turn himself in? He doesn't live with me anymore. I don't condone his lifestyle so we barely even talk."

Mr. Oliver shrugged. "Well, if you want your case to move forward, you'd better try to find him. This hanging over us will make things very difficult. As your attorney, my advice would be: give them what they want."

"Turn in my son," I repeated. "Will he be deported?"

"I don't know. It's either him or you. And since you have three other kids who need you, that would be a no-brainer for me." He grabbed his briefcase and stood. "But that's a choice you have to make on your own. Think about it. I'll come back tomorrow. We have to give the DA an answer. Honestly, I doubt I'll even be able to get you released unless you cooperate."

With that, he signaled for the guards to let him out.

I fell back against the wall, tears coming down my cheeks. I could go home. I might even get what I had worked so long for — citizenship — but what price would I have to pay?

CHAPTER 33

Fresh air had never smelled so good. I'd been locked up in that cage for two and a half weeks. And it had been the longest two and a half weeks of my life.

After Mr. Oliver left, I'd spent the next two days tossing and turning in my cell. Paco's sin had indeed made things worse for me. The guards were cruel and the inmates looked at me in disgust. The three-timer had stopped talking to me. But I held back until Rosa revealed that Alejandro had had another asthma attack — one that landed him in the ER. I didn't have a choice. I had to give the DA what he wanted.

Mr. Oliver drew up the paperwork. I was released on my own recognizance on a thirty-day Government Assist program, meaning the government needed my assistance to help solve a major crime.

All I had to do was hand them my son on a silver platter, and I could go live happily ever after.

What mother could live with that?

Though I had agreed to the DA's terms, I hadn't come to terms on whether that was something I could really do. How did a mother turn in her son when she knew it would alter his life forever?

Even if Paco was innocent, which I was still praying that he was, he would still be deported if he was arrested.

Savannah waved to me from the end of the hall. I really didn't want any cameras there, but I owed Savannah that much, so I had agreed to allow her to film me as I was being released today. Knowing the camera was rolling, I maintained a grateful smile.

She reached in and hugged me.

"I'm so glad that you're out," she said.

"Thanks to you. I can't wait to get home and hug my kids."

A thought seemed to occur to her, because the smile left her face and she shifted uncomfortably. "What's wrong?" I asked.

"We probably shouldn't go out the front."

"Why?"

"There are picketers out there," she said.

"Picketers for what?"

She sighed. "They're protesting you. The Anti-Immigration Foundation is fighting your release from jail. Some conservative

263

media pundits have picked up the story and" — she released a long pause — "let's just say it's not pretty. My sources are telling me that the White House may even make a comment on it."

"Oh, my God," I groaned. This nightmare would never end.

"But Oliver and Jerri are focused. While those protesters are focused on the bad son, they're going to play up the good son. I had a chance to sit and talk with Miguel and he is an amazing child."

"Yeah, but Miguel is an American citizen." My hands shook as I spoke. What had I gotten my family embroiled in?

"I know. But we want to contradict the picture the anti-immigration group is trying to paint of you as a mother. We want the courts to see the mother that is raising three wonderful U.S. citizens."

I fought back tears. Today was supposed to be a happy day. I couldn't let sorrow drown me.

Still, I said, "With these protesters, the judge could just deport me to make it all go away."

"If you didn't have your other children, I'd be worried," she admitted.

I bit back the thought that came to me: *That's easy for you to say.* I couldn't help but be worried when my future — when my children's future — was at stake.

"Yes, you have a battle ahead," Savannah continued, sensing my angst. "I don't know how this will end. But I'm faithful that it will all work out." She smiled knowingly at me. "A wise woman once told me things have a way of working themselves out."

I sighed. She was right. I didn't come this far to give up. I needed to hold on, because as bumpy as the ride was going to be, I had to remain faithful that it would all work out in the end.

CHAPTER 34

"Please just leave us alone!"

I slammed the phone down, then, after thinking about it, I snatched the cord out of the wall.

My phone had been ringing nonstop. Either they were calling about doing an interview with me or trying to get information about Paco.

I'd only been home forty-eight hours and the barrage was driving me crazy. My story had made Fox News and the vitriol of those commentators made me seem like the worst person to walk the face of the earth.

Yesterday, a reporter had accosted Miguel on the way home, and the mama bear in me almost attacked. Luckily, Rosa was there. She'd been amazing at helping me stay under control. She'd cursed the reporter out in Spanish and English, then shielded us both until we ran inside. I had to figure out an alternative way to get them to school, because we couldn't take too many more days like this.

"Mommy, I want to go outside and play," Alejandro said.

I guess I should've been grateful. Up until an hour ago, Alejandro or Maria wouldn't leave my side. "Sweetheart, we talked about this," I replied. I'd had to explain to them about the reporters.

He walked over to the front window and looked outside at the reporters camped in front of our house.

"But whyyy?" he whined.

"Because we're prisoners," Miguel snapped, joining his brother at the window.

"We're in jail like Mommy was," Maria added.

All of this — the whole scenario — was hurting my heart. I was grateful to be home, but I still felt like a prisoner. I'd decided I was going to try and just talk to Paco, maybe convince him to give himself up. That way I wouldn't have to live with the guilt of turning my eldest son in. The only problem was I had no idea how to find Paco. The number Miguel had called had been disconnected and I had no idea where he was staying.

I also had to check in with immigration officials once a week while my case made its way through the courts, but that was a small price to pay if it meant I no longer had to live in fear. Then again, it looked like I was still living in fear — fear of the unknown.

"Come here, kids," I said, patting the sofa next to me. "Have a seat. Let me talk to you guys."

Alejandro and Maria crawled around me. "I am so sorry you all are going through this." I wrapped my arms around them and relished their scents as they snuggled closer.

"Is it true what people are saying?" Miguel asked. He hadn't moved from the window, but he had turned to face me. "That we shouldn't be here and that Paco is a killer?"

I reached out for Miguel's hand. He paused, but then walked over and our fingers intertwined. "Sweetheart, don't listen to what people say. What do I tell you guys?"

Maria chimed in, "Sticks and stones can break my bones but words —"

"But these words do hurt," Miguel said, cutting her off. When he looked at me, he had tears in his eyes.

I pushed a loose thread of hair out of his face. "I understand that, son. And I can't apologize enough for that. It doesn't matter whether I belong here, the three of you do.

It is where you were born, so this is your home. This is where you will always live."

"But if they send you away, I want to come live with you," Maria said, hugging me tighter.

I struggled to fight back the tears. I'd thought about this all night. If I was forced to go back to Hidalgo, I couldn't take my children with me. My whole reason in coming to America had been to give them a better life. And I knew Rosa would step up to help me. I would just have to find a way to send her money to help raise them.

I couldn't believe I was planning a life without my kids. The thought of being without my children made a sickening feeling rise in my stomach.

"What are the chances of you being deported?" Miguel asked. He now stood upright, his man-of-the-house demeanor taking over. Miguel was so much like his father, inquisitive and thought-provoking and determined.

"Miguel, you let me worry about that, okay?"

"No, Mom," he replied with conviction. "This affects us all. So I think we should know what's going on."

I was about to protest when he continued. "You don't want me to wake up tomorrow and you're gone, and then we're left trying to figure out what to do. We have to develop a plan."

My thirteen-year-old was trying to come up with a plan in the event that I was deported. The tears I'd been fighting back trickled out. When I'd taken that long ride across the border all those years ago, I never imagined that one day I'd be here.

I took a deep breath, then explained to my son how their life would go on without me.

It had taken some time, but I'd gotten the kids settled in bed. I peeked outside. The camera crews had left, though I was sure they'd return with daylight. I let the curtain fall closed as I slumped down onto the sofa.

"Oh, Julio, my life is such a mess," I whispered. I wondered if he were here, what would he want us to do?

Then a thought struck me. If Julio were here, maybe things wouldn't be so bad. If my husband hadn't died, my son wouldn't be wanted for murder.

I was lost in thoughts of what if when I heard a light tapping on the back door. I sat up as the tapping got louder. I glanced over at the clock. It was just after midnight. If this was a dang reporter . . .

I walked over to the closet and retrieved Miguel's baseball bat. I then headed into the kitchen.

"Who is it?" I hissed.

"It's me, Ma."

The sound of my oldest son's voice made me swing the door open. My first reaction was relief. I wanted so desperately to take my son into my arms and just hold him. He looked worn down, like life on the streets had taken its toll. After a few seconds, I couldn't resist the urge. I took him into my arms, all but yanked him into the house, and then I hugged him as if my life depended on it.

"Mi hijo," I cried, plastering him with kisses.

Normally, he would've squirmed away, but it was as if he welcomed each kiss.

"Are you okay?" I asked, finally shutting the door and examining him from his head to the tips of his expensive tennis shoes.

He nodded. I peeked outside through the small window in the door.

"Don't worry, Ma," he said. "I made sure no one saw me."

I exhaled in relief, and then my eyes asked the question my mouth couldn't. And my son answered, "Mom, I didn't shoot the little girl . . ." He paused and let his words hang in the air. Finally, he added, "But I know who did and I have no idea what to do."

I wanted to tell him I knew what he should do — turn himself in. But I couldn't get the words to come out.

I knew all about the no-snitching creed of gangs, but our situation was bound by a different set of rules. Paco faced prison or deportation. I'd fled Hidalgo to keep the gangs from claiming my son. And now they'd taken him anyway. This story, no matter what happened — would not have a happy ending.

"Son, just come on in. Rest. We can talk about this tomorrow," I said.

My son's shoulders sagged in relief.

Chapter 35

The work visa has been granted for a year while your case makes its way through the system. So you have to find your son and give the DA what he wants.

Mr. Oliver's words were still playing in my head as I stood with my hand on the phone. He'd called just as we sat down to eat dinner.

I didn't kid myself — this wasn't going to be an easy journey. But at least I was out of the shadows. It had taken nineteen years, and while my faith had wavered, it had never faltered. And I was reaping the fruits of my patience. But I couldn't rejoice, not when my eldest son's fate hung in the wind.

I hadn't told Mr. Oliver that Paco was here. I needed to talk to my son first.

"Pass the tamales!" Miguel's voice snapped me back to the dining room of our tiny home. My family was squished around our small dining room table, but I'd never seen anything more beautiful in my life.

"Miguel, wipe your mouth, son," I said, returning to the table and pointing to the tamale crumbs all around his lips.

"Sorry," he said, using his sleeve to wipe them off. "These tamales . . . yes, *son deliciosos!*"

That brought a smile to my face. "That's right, *mi hijo,* they're *deliciosos.*"

He winked at me and my heart filled with joy. There was nothing like being deprived of your family to make you appreciate your family.

Yet it was my love for my family that had my stomach in knots. The unknown was a terrible place to be.

"So Mom has you speaking Spanish now, Miguel?" Paco joked. "You're American, homie."

I playfully popped Paco on the arm. And he howled like I had really hurt him, which made the whole table erupt in laughter. There had been a hostage situation at a nearby school, so the media had moved on and there were no reporters camped out today. That had allowed us all to relax just a little bit.

"You can love America and not forget your roots," I reminded him.

"Yeah, yeah, yeah," he chuckled.

"Here, eat up," I said, plopping some more black beans onto his plate.

"Mom, I'm stuffed," Paco said, rubbing his stomach.

"You're skin and bones." I squeezed his arm. "Eat for me."

"Yeah," Alejandro chimed in. "It's a party!"

I pointed the serving utensil in his direction. "Which is the only reason I'm letting you eat your cake with dinner."

I took my finger and dipped it in his icing, then tapped his nose. Alejandro giggled.

I wished we could live in this temporary utopia forever. My whole family gathered together. The problems that plagued us, momentarily forgotten.

The kids had been so happy to see Paco when they'd awakened this morning. Paco had played with them, then crashed like he hadn't slept in days. He'd finally awakened about an hour ago — just in time to join us for dinner.

I started my job at the Freedom Coalition tomorrow, and for the first time since I'd entered the United States, I was legal, even if it was temporary. Mr. Oliver was confident that because of my unblemished past, my future looked bright — if we could work out this thing with Paco. If I could convince my son to tell the police what they needed to know.

"So, Paco, how's life?" I asked, taking a seat next to him.

"It's okay, Ma," he said. "Matter of fact," he reached into his pocket and pulled out a wad of money and slid it across the table, "go buy yourself something nice for your first day at work."

My first instinct was to chastise him. But I didn't want this day ruined or to push Paco away.

"No, son. I can't accept this."

"I'll take it!" Miguel said, reaching across the table to pick up the money.

I popped Miguel's hand, then took the money, forced my smile back on my face, and turned to Paco. "No, son. I want you to start a savings account for yourself. One day you may need this money."

I knew that with Paco's situation, there was no way he'd go near a bank, but I had to figure out a way to refuse his ill-gotten money without making him angry.

It took everything inside me not to preach to Paco. But he wasn't ready to receive the Word. I had turned him over to God, so I knew at some point, he'd be handled. This past month had taught me that things didn't come when we wanted them, but if we stayed faithful, they'd come in due time.

Luckily, the sound of the chiming doorbell interrupted us.

"That's probably Rosa," I said, standing and heading to the door.

"Are you guys eating without me?" my cheery friend said as she entered.

Her kids raced past me. "Ooooh, Mommy, they're eating cake," her youngest announced when she saw Alejandro and Maria.

"Can you two not be rude and say hello to Ms. Anna?" Rosa chastised.

"Hi, Ms. Anna," they sang in unison, then turned back to their mother. "Can we have cake?"

Rosa raised an eyebrow at me. "Cake? Really?"

"It's a celebration." I flashed a smile.

"I guess you're right." She held up two bottles of wine. "And I brought the good stuff to celebrate."

"Cake, Mommy? Please?" Rosa's oldest repeated.

"Go ahead," Rosa replied to her children's gleeful excitement.

Rosa and I headed into the kitchen. She put one bottle of wine in the refrigerator, then unscrewed the top on the other. "I'm so glad those reporters are gone," she said.

"For now," I replied.

"Are you ready for your new job?" she asked.

"I am. I'm so excited to be fighting for immigration. I don't belittle any job I've ever had, and I'm grateful for the Markham, but I think this will be so much more fulfilling."

Rosa nodded as she removed two glasses from the cabinet.

"I'm sure it will be. And I am still trying to understand how the woman who gets in trouble lands the dream job."

I laughed as she filled both glasses. "And this is a dream. It's a little more money, not a lot. But it's a calling. I am so happy."

"I'm happy, too. Because this couldn't happen to a better woman." She hugged me. "I think I need some of your faith."

"Says the woman with two glasses of wine in her hand."

"What? Jesus drank wine. Besides, one of these is for you." Rosa handed me a glass, then raised hers in a toast.

"To the most faithful woman I know. May we all strive for a little bit of that," she said.

We clinked glasses, then took a sip of the wine. After a few seconds, Rosa glanced over her shoulder toward the dining room, then lowered her voice. "I guess since you got Paco here, he agreed to help the police?" she whispered.

"No, I didn't get him here. He showed up on his own. And actually, I haven't been able to get up the nerve to talk to him."

"Really, Anna?" Rosa said. "He's your child. Why are you acting like you're scared of him?"

I set my glass on the counter. "I'm not scared. I just don't want to push him away."

She put her glass on the counter as well and took a step toward me, her hands on her hips to let me know that she meant business. "Well, you can't keep your head in the sand. And how long is he here? You're jeopardizing your own status. And you have those other three kids to think about."

"So what am I supposed to do?"

Before Rosa could finish, Paco appeared in the doorway. My house was small and judging by the look on his face, I was sure he'd heard everything even though we'd kept our voices low.

"Ma . . ." he said.

Rosa looked back and forth between us, then said, "Let me go check on my kids. They're probably eating up all the cake." She grabbed her wineglass and headed out.

"I'm sorry, Ma," Paco said.

Instinct took over and I pulled my boy

into my arms and squeezed him tight. Tears popped into my eyes when he squeezed me back.

I took a step back, cupped his face in my hands. "Tell me what happened. The truth. You didn't do what they said, right? You had nothing to do with killing that little girl?" I asked.

He looked me in the eye, his tears matching mine. "No, I told you," he said, and my heart sank in relief because I believed him. "But I was with the guy who did. He wasn't trying to hurt that little girl."

"Oh, Paco," I said, hugging him again. "You've got to go to the police. Tell them everything they need to know. You're a wanted man. You can't run forever."

"I don't want to go to jail."

My heart ached as I thought: even if he was able to avoid being charged with the crime, he would still be deported. I wondered if he even realized that was an option. So while I wanted him to turn himself in, I knew that, regardless, he'd either be led to jail or to the border.

Both options broke my heart.

"I have a good immigration attorney. Maybe he could . . ." I couldn't even finish the sentence because I didn't believe there was anything Mr. Oliver could do. But just as quickly as the doubt set in, I reminded myself of how my faith had just pulled me through the most trying of times.

"Sweetheart, this is all going to work out," I told him. "I don't know how, but it will." I took a deep breath. "You can't stay on the run. You have to turn yourself in and tell the police what you know. Help them find the real killer."

Paco nodded, though his shoulders sank in defeat. "Ma, I promise, I'm gonna make this up to you. I'm gonna leave when it gets dark, gonna tie up some loose ends, then I'll turn myself in. I heard what Ms. Rosa said. I don't want this to mess you up. You have to be here for Alejandro, Miguel, and Maria."

That brought more tears to my eyes. All this time I had felt like Paco was being selfish, but my son was sacrificing himself for his family.

This was both the happiest and saddest day of my life.

■ ■ ■ ■

TREY

■ ■ ■ ■

CHAPTER 36

Everyone knew that when it came to gangs, there was only one way out. That's why I'd tried my best to steer clear of the 713 Crips, the notorious gang in my Fifth Ward neighborhood. But while I didn't want to have anything to do with the gang, they wanted everything to do with me.

My best friend, Wiz, was the only other boy in my neighborhood I knew that felt like me — and didn't want anything to do with the gangs. The third member of our crew — this dude named Paco — didn't care for the gangs, either, but he'd adapted a lot better than me and Wiz.

We all had been sucked in with seemingly no way out. That's why the three of us were sitting here on the corner of Lyons and Lockwood Boulevard, doing Monster's dirty work.

Monster was the leader of the 713 Crips, and he'd helped each of us out at one point by loaning us money for our families. We'd been paying the price ever since.

At eighteen, I already knew this thug life wasn't for me. I just wanted out of the game. I didn't want to be sitting on a corner pushing black market guns. I didn't want this to be my life. It had been my past. I didn't want it to be my future. But I didn't see any other ending for my story.

Wiz leaned back against the building, an old, boarded-up gas station where we did a lot of our business. His eyes were a window into a soul that also wanted to be anywhere but here.

I'd met Wiz when we were both ten-year-olds who had been dumped at the local Boys & Girls Club by our parents. We'd spent every moment outside of school there, and our mentor, Mr. Graham, tried his best to keep us on the straight and narrow. We'd met Paco two years later when his mom started sending him there in hopes that he'd like it better than the streets. But by age fourteen, the streets had summoned all of us, and now we were obligated to do Monster's bidding.

"Paco, man, what's wrong with you?" Wiz asked. Paco had been acting weird since we'd gotten out here. He'd been pacing back and forth and jumping at every little sound.

"Yeah, bruh, you've been walking back and forth and looking over your shoulder. You're gonna draw attention to us, acting all suspect like that," I said.

Paco stopped in his tracks and turned to us. "I gotta tell y'all something."

The fear across his face made us both stand up straight.

"What's up?" Wiz said.

Paco shifted his weight from one foot to the other. He ran his hands back and forth through his curly black hair. Then he said, "Well, ah, so y'all heard about the shooting a couple of weeks ago at the Main Event in Stafford, where that little girl was killed?"

"Dude, what are you talking about?" Wiz said.

"The six-year-old. She was killed and her sister was injured. Then ICE turned around and picked up her mother. Now they're deporting the mom."

Wiz shook his head like he had no idea what Paco was talking about. But I nodded. I'd heard about it at home. I lived with my grandmother's friend, and she was always watching TV and that story had been breaking news.

"Yeah," I said. "I know the story. What

about it?"

When Paco lowered his eyes in shame, I said, "Oh snap, was that you?"

Paco slowly nodded. "Kinda. Monster wanted us to take out these two dudes, and we followed them to the Main Event." He got choked up. "It was me and Little Will . . . you know that dude is crazy. When the guys walked out, Little Will just started firing. I had my piece out but just to scare the dudes. I had no idea Little Will was just gonna start blazin'. The little girl . . ." He choked back his words.

I had no idea that was a Monster shooting, but I should've known. If blood was shed in this city, Monster was likely to be behind it.

We were all silent. I know Paco was dying inside, because I would be, too. We ran guns. We weren't killers.

"What did Monster say?" I asked. "You know about killing the kid and the mom getting deported?"

Paco shook his head. "Called them casualties of war. He didn't even think twice about them. He was madder that we let the guys get away."

Casualties of war.

Monster was the evilest man I'd ever met.

"Yo, but the news said the cops know who

did it," I said. The expression on Paco's face made my heart jump.

"Dude, are you for real?" Wiz shouted. "You're out here with us and the heat is on you?"

"Man, I gotta get some money to get out of town," Paco said. "The DA is tryin' to get my mom to turn on me."

"What?" I said. "They're trying to get your mom to snitch on you? How do you know?"

"I overheard her the other day talking to her friend about it," he said as he began that pacing again. "Plus, Little Will is missing."

"Missing?" I said.

Paco nodded. "Yeah, ain't nobody seen him and y'all know Monster. He was pretty pissed about us missing those dudes."

"So, um, you scared?" Wiz asked the question I know all of us were thinking. When Monster sent you on a mission and you not only failed, but you brought unnecessary heat, you became expendable.

Killing a kid was definitely unnecessary heat.

"Nah," Paco said. "Monster said we were straight." The way his voice quavered, we all knew that was a lie.

"You know what?" Paco said. "I shouldn't

have said nothin'. I was just, you know, let-
tin' y'all know. I'm going to take a piss."

He disappeared around the back of the
store. When he was out of earshot, Wiz said,
"You know Monster is gonna get him,
right?"

I couldn't say anything because I knew
my friend was right. But what could we do
about it?

Wiz bit down on his bottom lip, something
he did whenever he was deep in thought.
Finally, he leaned in and lowered his voice.
"Can I tell you something?"

With his bifocal glasses and freckled skin,
Wiz had struggled to find his place. Half-
black, half-white, he never quite felt like he
fit in anywhere. And since I had left a
mother who spent her days drugging and
running after various men, we had immediately bonded. So I could tell when
something was bothering him, and the look
on his face told me it was more than just
Paco's revelation.

"Yeah, man. What's up?" I asked.

He was silent, like he was unsure whether
he should say something.

"Just spit it out," I said. While Wiz was
reserved with everyone else, with me he
always spoke his mind.

"I got accepted to Jarvis." He rushed the

290

words out.

"What is Jarvis?" I asked.

"College," he whispered like it was a bad word.

"College!"

Wiz leaned up, looked nervously around. "Shhh, man. I don't want no one to know that. Not even Paco."

I lowered my voice. "For real? You going to college?" I asked. I knew Wiz wanted a different life, but I didn't know that life involved college.

"Yeah, I've been working with Mr. G. Apparently, the Boys & Girls Club has some kind of partnership with Jarvis Christian College."

"Wait, hol' up. Christian? So you're going to learn how to be a minister or something?"

"That's just the name of it," he said, like I was the dumb one in this friendship. "They got some kind of grant that's supposed to get more black males to go to college."

"Wow, and Mr. G. wanted you?" I wasn't jealous, I was happy for my boy. But just the thought of Wiz getting out of the game made me feel some kind of way.

"He wanted *us*. But remember, I tried to get you to go with me to see him last month when you had to go see your brother? Mr. G. said he called you a couple of times,

291

and you never called him back."

I groaned as I remembered that I had forgotten to return his call. He'd left me a message, but when I heard him mention college, I'd just deleted it.

I'd barely graduated from high school. I never even thought about college. Though my teachers — and Mr. G. — used to always encourage me to go, saying I was naturally intelligent. But in my world, college was just a dream. In my world, it was all about survival. Wiz was from the same world, and if I felt like I didn't belong, Wiz was even more of an outcast. He and I were in the same boat now, parentless and on our own. We did everything in our power to keep our distance from the Crips and only did our small hustles for Monster because we didn't really have a choice.

"I can't believe you're going off to college," I said.

"What? You think I'm supposed to stay around here doing this for the rest of my life?" His voice was filled with disgust as he glanced around the dilapidated parking lot. The raggedy, broken gas pumps still said $1.67 a gallon. That's how long this place had been closed.

I shrugged. "Nah, man. I get what you're saying. I'm just . . . I guess I'm just shocked."

"I just wanna bounce," he said. "Get out of this grind."

"Wow," I repeated, only because I didn't know what else to say. "College," I said, leaning back, still stunned.

"Yeah, man," Wiz said. Then he smiled like he was thinking of that better life. "I might go up there and get me one of those college chicks. I might even become a Q-Dog or a Kappa, like Mr. G."

"Man, I can't see you as one of those sorority people," I laughed.

"*Fraternity,* man," Wiz said. "Sororities are for girls."

I shrugged. It's not like I would know any of that. My mother had been a high school dropout. My grandmother had been a middle school dropout. I didn't need to go to college and be a college dropout. Especially since I'd done good to finish high school last year. Besides, I had one focus and one focus only. Getting that paper and getting my life right, so I could get my little brother.

"Well, whatever. I'm happy for you." I meant that. As bad as I wanted a change for me, I wanted my boy to be happy as well.

"I'm gonna just disappear," Wiz continued. He was smiling like he was leaving tomorrow. "I'm letting you know now. I love you, man, but I ain't even goin' to tell you when I'm leavin'. The less you know, the better. That way, when Monster and his crew come looking for me, you can honestly say you don't know nothin'."

I groaned. Now I wished he hadn't told me which college he was going to. That way I would be telling the truth that I didn't know where Wiz was.

Paco emerged from around the corner, and Wiz immediately changed the subject.

"How's your little bro?" Wiz asked me.

My little brother, Jamal, was the reason I hadn't left Houston myself.

"He's a'ight. Sad all the time."

"Shoot, I don't blame him." Wiz shook his head. "I hate they put him in the system."

"You and me both."

My eight-year-old brother had been sent to foster care after my grandmother died nine months ago. Because I was eighteen, I was able to be out on my own. But the state wouldn't let me have custody of my little brother like I wanted because, as the social worker said, "You aren't stable enough."

My dad had been in a gang — and gunned down when I was just three. My mom had held us together until her new boyfriend —

Jamal's father — got her hooked on drugs right after Jamal was born. She disappeared a few years ago, and Jamal and I were with Grams after that.

Then Gram's death had split us up for good.

"Y'all ain't got no uncles or aunts or nobody that can take him?" Paco interjected.

That both pained me and pissed me off. "My triflin' uncle is the only halfway decent person, but he doesn't want to have anything to do with Jamal, talking about he's a bachelor. My mama had a cousin, but she's on drugs, too. So, nah, Grams was the last person we had."

I got nostalgic thinking about my grandmother. Everyone always asked what she died from. She was old. Real old. She had been forty-five when she had my mom. And despite her hard life, she woke up every morning with a smile on her face, singing some spiritual song. I felt myself tearing up as I heard her voice singing "Amazing Grace" and reading her old, torn Bible. I'd bought her a new one for Christmas, but she kept that raggedy one, saying a Bible that's falling apart usually belongs to someone that isn't. Remembering that brought a pang to my heart.

I was grateful when Wiz spoke, so I could push aside thoughts of Grams.

"Yo, Paco, let me ask you something. You tired of this?" He motioned around the empty parking lot.

I expected Paco to pledge his loyalty to the streets, but he said, "Between the three of us? Hell, yeah. But what else we got?"

"You got a mama," I said. "You could go home."

He looked like he was thinking. "Go home to what?" he replied. "Poverty? Nah. My mom's bitchin' every day? Unh-unh."

"Least you got a moms that cares," Wiz said.

Paco shrugged. "I ain't about that strugglin' life. I was just at my mom's crib last week, when I heard her talking to her friend. I felt claustrophobic with all of us up in that tiny place. Just gotta deal with the bad because the good is good, ya know?"

I knew. Monster's money was the only way the three of us had been surviving. But the cost we were paying was starting to take its toll.

Monster was Suge Knight, Nino Brown, and Michael Corleone rolled into one. Not only was he scary — just from his towering six-foot-four, three-hundred-pound presence — but he was ruthless. Word around the neighborhood was that his mama had given him his name because he was a monster from the day he was born. Though no one ever said anything negative to Monster's face, almost everyone I knew hated him.

Wiz sighed. "I don't think this dude is gonna show," he said.

We'd been waiting on this college kid who was coming to pick up a piece. He hadn't shown up and we'd been waiting for forty-five minutes.

"Let's just get out of here," Wiz said.

"Man, Monster is gonna be trippin' if we don't get rid of these pieces. We're supposed to bring him two Gs. We're five hundred dollars short," I said. I thought about telling them about the extra two hundred dollars I'd gotten from the old man outside the gun store the other day. But I'd already put that money up, hidden it in my bootleg savings account — under my mattress. While most of the guys I knew used their money to splurge on the latest gear and hottest jewelry, outside of a pair of Jordans, I didn't spend a dime. I held on to my money like it was a vital organ. My hope was that one day, I'd have enough money to get my brother and leave this life.

"What are we supposed to do then?" Wiz snapped. "Put an ad on Craigslist? Ain't nobody buyin' today."

My friend was right and I was tired. Plus, I needed to get over to the group home so that I could see Jamal before it was too late. I'd been trying to make a point of going over there every other day, just to give him some sense of normalcy.

"Yeah, he's right. Let's hit up another spot, see if we can move some stuff there," Paco said.

Paco grabbed the duffel bag where we had the guns stored, and threw the bag over his shoulder. We were about to get into Wiz's beat-up Impala when, out of nowhere, two guys sped alongside of us and jumped out the car.

"Give me your money!" one of the guys said. He was wearing a low-cut baseball hat that hid his face.

Wiz immediately jumped back. "We ain't got no money."

"Don't play, or I'll bust a cap in you," the guy said, thrusting a gun in Wiz's face. "Give me the money *and* the guns."

No. No. No. The last thing we needed was to get robbed of Monster's money *and* his guns.

The second robber, a much taller, linebacker-looking dude, pointed at the duffel bag on Paco's shoulder.

"Hand it over, homie."

Paco looked to me, then to Wiz. We both stood in horror as Paco pulled the bag close to him and then said, "Nah, homie. You gon' have to shoot me."

"You ain't said nothing but a word," the guy said.

Before I could ask Paco if he had lost his mind, the sound of a single gunshot pierced the night.

I was too stunned to scream, and Wiz and I watched in horror as Paco hit the ground.

The first guy turned to me. "Which one of y'all is next?"

I could not believe we were about to go out like this. My chest heaved. I didn't know what a panic attack was, but I was sure that I was having one this very moment.

"Here," Wiz said, thrusting the money at the guy. "This all we got."

I kept struggling to breathe as I thought about my brother. He'd lost our mother, our grandmother. Was he about to lose me, too?

"Yo, let's roll," the guy who'd shot Paco said. He'd picked up the duffel bag and slung it over his shoulder.

Satisfied with the wad, the first guy stuffed the money in his pockets. Then the two of them jumped in the car and sped off. Wiz and I looked at each other, on the verge of tears.

I looked down at Paco as I struggled to contain my breathing.

Wiz pulled my arm. "Come on, man. We gotta go."

"W-we're just gonna leave him?" I cried.

"We don't have any choice. He's dead! If the cops come, we gotta answer questions."

Wiz didn't wait for me. He just jumped in his car. After a few seconds he rolled down the window and said, "Come on, Trey. We gotta go, now!"

I stumbled to the car, swung the passenger door open, and fell into the seat.

Paco. Was. Dead.

And we'd lost Monster's money and his guns.

That meant it was just a matter of time before we were dead, too.

CHAPTER 37

We had been pacing in this old abandoned warehouse all night and neither Wiz nor I had come up with any ideas about what we were going to do.

"Man, I say we find someone else to rob," Wiz said. We both were sick about Paco, and at some point I knew that the pain of losing our friend would hit me like a bulldozer. But right now I was in survival mode.

I cocked my head and looked at him. "Dude, there's a reason we out here as corner stumpers," I told him. "We're not stickup kids."

Wiz and I sold guns, but neither of us had ever used one.

"Then what are we supposed to do?" Wiz said, running his hand over his head. We both had dozed off and on, but the lack of real sleep was evident in both of our faces.

Wiz knew I was right. He and I weren't true criminals. We were just trying to survive. We were making it day to day. If we had our way, neither one of us would have anything to do with gangs. But Monster wasn't in the business of letting people have their way. We'd just been grateful that he hadn't made us get in the drug game, since both of us had lost parents to drugs. But we'd come to discover that running guns was a whole lot worse. This gun game was big money, and Wiz and I had just lost not only the money but the guns.

"What do you think Monster is gonna do?" Wiz said. His tone was hushed like he was afraid of the rats overhearing or something.

"Put a bullet in both of our heads," I replied in all seriousness. "He ain't gon' care about Paco. All he cares about is his bread."

Wiz slid to the ground.

We had to figure out something and figure it out quick. Wiz had called Monster's henchman Don and told him what happened. Of course, Don wasn't trying to hear it. Wiz put him on speakerphone, and all I heard was "Y'all little punks better have our money by ten o'clock. If you don't, I'ma have your blood. Word is bond." Then he hung up, and Wiz and I had been running ever since.

If there was one thing that we knew about Monster and his crew, it was that they didn't make idle threats. If they said they were gonna put a bullet in your head, you better believe you'd have a hole in your head.

"We gotta run. We gotta get out of town," Wiz said.

"Man, I can't leave my brother. He won't have anybody," I said.

"Well, he won't have anybody when Monster kills you so . . ."

With that thought fear spread throughout my body. I paced across the warehouse, stopping only as a rat scurried past, paused, then stared at me like we were invading his space, before continuing into the wall.

"Isn't there any other option?" I said, because staying in this rat-infested place wasn't one.

"No, you know with Monster there are only two options: have his money or die."

"You don't think we can talk to Monster?" I asked.

"Does Monster look like he's in the 'let's discuss this' business?"

He was right about that. The last guy that had come up short with Monster had tried to "talk" to him, and before he finished his first sentence, Monster's goons cut off his tongue.

Still, I said, "Look, I say we just tell the truth. They know that we were robbed. We just need to tell Monster that we're gonna get his money and we just need time."

"I say we run," Wiz said. "Because even if he agrees to that, he's gonna add on his fifty percent late payment penalty. Where would we get that money from?"

I was beyond frustrated. "All I know is, I can't run. Plus, how far can your whip even get us? To the county line?"

"I know your car is so much better . . . Oh, wait, you don't have a car," he snapped.

"Look, I don't want to fight. We're stressed. We just gotta handle this. So I'm gonna go talk to Monster, man to man."

I was headed toward the door when Wiz came running after me.

I'd been living with an old friend of my grandmother's, Ms. Laura, but I couldn't take this drama to her doorstep. Even still, I wanted to go see how much money I had hidden in my mattress so I could know what to say to Monster.

"Let's just run by my crib," I said as we walked outside. "I've been saving some money. It ain't what we owe, but it'll be something, and maybe Monster will give us time to work off the rest." My heart sank at the thought of giving Monster my money. But it was better than giving him my life.

"I don't know, man," Wiz said, shaking his head. "I'm ready to just bounce."

"Let's just try this first," I said.

We dipped into the alley where Wiz had parked his car, hopped in, then headed to my house, which I hated because there were like eight people living there, including Ms. Laura's trifling thirty-year-old grandson, Carl, who made it his business to make my life miserable.

"Hey, boy. Where you been?" Ms. Laura said when I came through the door. Her soap opera was blaring in the background.

"Just out," I replied.

"Little fake gangsta always out," Carl said, sitting at the kitchen table, playing solitaire, which he did all day, every day.

I just ignored him. I'd learned that was the best way to handle all of Ms. Laura's relatives. Because they always reminded me that I was just an "outside charity case." I went into my room and slipped underneath my mattress. I had cut a hole in the middle of the mattress and stuffed a sock with my money. I stuck my hand in the hole, reached around, and didn't feel anything. My heart immediately began to race. I pulled the twin-sized mattress off the bed, flipped it over, and dug and dug. Before long, I realized my money was gone.

I raced back into the living room. "Ms. Laura, Ms. Laura!"

"What is it, boy?" she said, sitting up from her spot on the sofa. "Calm your nerves."

"I had some money and it's missing," I huffed.

"You had some money?" she said. "Money for what?"

"I've been saving it to help my brother, and now it's gone."

The smirk on her grandson's face told me exactly where my money had gone.

I spun toward him. "Did you touch my money, Carl?"

"What it look like?" he said.

I don't know what came over me, but I dove across the table. Carl had about four inches on me, but in that moment I didn't care. "Where is my money? Give me my money back," I said as I pummeled him.

I knocked him over onto the floor, but as soon as he got his bearings, he threw me off like I was a rag doll.

Ms. Laura was screaming. "What in tarnation? If you two don't stop it!"

"Grandma, you better get this little punk before I have to hurt him," Carl said as he picked his chair up.

"You ain't gonna hurt nobody," she said.

"He stole my money!" I screamed, stumbling as I pulled myself up off the floor.

"I don't know what you're talking about." He plopped back down in his seat and went back to playing his card game.

"You're a liar!" I screamed.

Ms. Laura placed her hands on her robust hips and planted herself firmly between us. "Look, if Carl said he ain't seen the money, then he ain't seen your money," she said.

"He's lying. He's a thief."

"He paid his debt to society," Ms. Laura said.

It was frustrating because Carl had done two stints for armed robbery, and Ms. Laura still didn't believe he was capable of any wrongdoing.

"I just need my money back. I really need my money back," I cried, my anger gone. Desperation was in its place.

"What you need money for so bad?" she said. "Are you in some sort of trouble? You know you can't bring no trouble up in here." She wagged her finger at me.

"Ms. Laura, please."

Carl shook his head as he turned over cards. "Grandma, I always told you about doing these charity cases."

"Ain't nobody talking to you," I screamed.

Carl leaned back, smugness filling his face. "Look, li'l man, I understand. You're upset about a few hundred dollars missing."

"How did you know how much it was?"

Ms. Laura cut her eyes as if she wanted to know the answer to that herself.

He shrugged. "I don't know. I just assumed if you had money, that's how much it is."

"Liar!" I screamed.

"Enough," Ms. Laura said. "Unless you got some proof that Carl stole your money, you're not going to come in my house accusing my grandson."

I knew that this was useless. More than that, I was done with this place. I stomped back into my room, grabbed my old Nike bag, and stuffed as much as I could into it. Then I stomped back through the living room.

"Now, Trey, where you going? Why are you being so dramatic?"

"Li'l dude always dramatic," Carl said.

I ignored both of them as I stomped back outside.

"Don't stay gone too long," Ms. Laura called out after me. "I'm making some peach cobbler."

I ignored her and let the screen door slam

on the sound of her voice.

I walked down the sidewalk to see Wiz under the hood of his car. He glanced at me, then turned his attention back to the car. "Man, this crap overheated. I can't believe this piece of . . ." His words trailed off as he took in the expression on my face. "Uh, what's up?" His eyes drifted down to my duffel bag. "Did you get the money?" he asked.

I shook my head. "Man, it's gone." For the first time since my grandmother died, I felt real tears seep out.

Wiz's eyes bucked. "What do you mean, it's gone?"

"The money's gone." I swallowed the lump in my throat. "Somebody stole it."

"Oh, snap. So now what are we gonna do?"

I was just about to answer him when I saw Monster's henchmen driving down the street toward the house. The car was moving slowly like in one of those gangster movies. Wiz and I looked at each other, and then, without saying a word, we both took off running.

CHAPTER 38

Forty-eight hours.

That's how long Wiz and I had been hiding out in the abandoned warehouse. Out of all the times for Wiz's raggedy car to break . . . I mean, I didn't think it would get us far, but I at least thought it would get us out of the neighborhood. Now we had no transportation, no money, and no hope.

We'd managed to scrounge up some food, but I was ready to go. We'd heard that Monster's boys were still looking for us. Terry, one of his runners and a friend from the hood, had told us when we went out to find something to eat last night. Wiz didn't need to convince me not to talk to Monster, because at this point, we both knew there was no talking. The jacked-up part about all of this was that we were the ones that were robbed, but Monster didn't care about the why. If you had his product, you were responsible for his product.

"You think . . ." I paused before putting into words the thoughts that had been on my mind since the shooting. "Do you think Monster sent those dudes to shoot Paco?"

Wiz shrugged. "I don't know. I thought about that. But why would he steal his own product?"

"To put us on the hook for it," I replied.

At this point the worry had worn Wiz down. His eyes were puffy and red. We'd been sleeping on the floor for the past two days, so that, coupled with not knowing if we were going to walk outside and get blasted, was taking its toll.

We sat in silence, then he lit up and said, "Look, man, I'm about to get some money. That'll buy some kind of way to get out of town."

"Where are you going to get it from?" I asked.

"I called Portia," he said, referring to his on-again, off-again girlfriend. "She said her mom has a couple pieces I may be able to pawn. It should be enough for one bus ticket." He looked at me and I knew what that meant. My boy was about to bounce. I would be on my own.

"Nah, man. I get it," I told him. "You do what you gotta do."

I could tell this was a decision he'd been wrestling with. And I should've known something was up because he'd spent an hour last night on the phone with Portia. Usually, Wiz had no problem talking to her in front of me, but he took the conversation to the back of the warehouse.

"I'm sorry, man," Wiz continued. "It's just . . . I have dreams . . . and running from Monster the rest of my life is a nightmare. Working for Monster the rest of my life ain't it. Portia is the only tie I have here, and she ain't even somebody I want to spend the rest of my life with, so I need to just go. I should've been gone. You know I don't share this with nobody but you. But this ain't the life I want. I wanna go and be somebody. I want a life that my family didn't even dream of."

The anguish in his voice made me sad. At least I had Jamal. Wiz had one brother on death row. His other brother had been killed when we were twelve, and his parents had both overdosed.

"Nah, B. I feel you," I replied.

I'd long given up on my dreams. My only dream now was to get to a point where I could take care of my brother so that he didn't grow up in the foster care system. Because the chances of a little black boy being adopted were slim to none, and slim didn't visit our hood.

"Well, look," I told him, "I'll roll with you over to Portia's. Maybe she can get us something to eat because I'm starving. And then we'll split up."

"What are you gonna do?"

I shrugged. "I'll figure something out. You don't have to worry about me."

"You sure you ain't mad?" he asked.

"Nah, man. Not at you."

I couldn't be mad. If I didn't have my little brother, I'd be long gone, too. We gave each other the brother hug and then headed out the door. We took back alleys and out-of-the-way sidewalks, headed to Portia's house. She lived in Fifth Ward, too. But by the time we finished dipping and darting down all these alternate routes, it had taken us almost an hour to get to her house. As soon as we got to her door, she waved us around to the back.

"What kind of trouble y'all in?" she hissed as she looked up and down the street to make sure we hadn't been followed. She quickly closed the door, then pulled the curtains shut. "Word on the street is that Monster is after y'all."

"Bae, I told you, we got robbed," Wiz said, planting a quick kiss on her lips. "Somebody stole Monster's money and guns, and now we on the hook for it."

Fear filled her face. Portia grew up in the hood, too, so she knew what happened to people that messed with Monster's money. "Dang," she said. "I'm sorry to hear that. But what y'all gonna do?" She ran her burgundy braids around her fingers, like she was trying to calm her nerves.

"I'm just gonna get what you told me you can get for me and then I'm out," Wiz said.

"Okay," she said, reaching into her pocket, then handing him a handful of jewelry. "I don't know how much you can get for it. Most of it is just costume stuff. But a few pieces are from when my mom used to date that drug dealer. So they ought to be worth a little bit." She stared Wiz in the eye. "You know how I feel about this, though, Wiz."

He leaned in and kissed her again. "I love you, baby. I'm sorry. I'm gonna just put it in the pawnshop, and I promise you, I'm gonna send you the money to get it out."

"You better," she said. " 'Cause my mama will kill me if she finds this out." Portia's mother was in Los Angeles, taking care of her grandmother, so I guessed Portia was hoping she could have the jewelry back before her mother returned.

"Well, I appreciate it. You could be saving

314

my life, Bae," Wiz said. In that moment I wished that I had taken the time to have a girl. But my entire focus had been on Jamal, and the few chicks I hung with were nothing serious.

"Hey, Portia, you got anything to eat?" I asked her. "We're kinda hungry."

"Kinda is a big understatement," Wiz said.

She looked at me and nodded her head. "Yeah, there's some bologna in there I was frying. Y'all want a sandwich?"

She might as well have said she had a T-bone steak grilling. A bologna sandwich sounded delicious.

"Word. I'll take a couple," I said.

"Y'all gonna have to take them to go, though, because . . ." She didn't even have to finish her sentence as she headed to the kitchen. We all knew that Monster's bullets had no name. So as long as he was looking for us, she didn't want to become a statistic.

We followed her into the kitchen. She quickly made us sandwiches, wrapped them in plastic wrap, then threw that, along with some chips, fruit, and cheese, into a brown paper bag. Even though she was helping, I could tell Portia wanted us out of her house as fast as possible. And of course, I couldn't blame her.

"Be careful, Bae," she told Wiz as she

walked us to the door.

He kissed her again, this time a lot more passionately. I wondered if she knew this would be her last time seeing him.

"I will, and I'll call you when I get where I'm going."

"Where are you going?" she asked once we were on the other side of the door.

"I'm not going to tell you that." They stared at each other, and she just nodded in understanding.

"I love you," Wiz said.

"I love you, too," she replied. "Trey, you be careful."

We made our way back around to the front of the house. I was just about to tell Wiz goodbye when a familiar Cutlass came rolling by. We knew it was Don's because of the extended spinners and loud royal-blue paint, which only he had. Before either of us could say a word, the window rolled down. We took off running down the side alley and the car gave chase. I went one direction; Wiz went the other. But I knew he was fleeing just like me — as if his life depended on it.

I had never felt such fear. Images of my mom . . . of Jamal . . . my grandmother . . . all of those shot through my head.

Please, God, just let me live!

When I heard tires screech, I stopped running. I was out of breath as I turned toward the sound. I was able to see that the Cutlass had come to a stop in front of the alley where Wiz had run.

That alley was a dead end.

I stood frozen, trying to debate what to do. And then I heard it:

Pop. Pop. Pop.

Those three gunshots would stay with me forever. I knew that Wiz was gone. When I heard the tires screech again, I took off. I ran, jumped a fence, then ran again.

I approached the Metro bus stop just as a bus was coming. I remembered my Metro pass in my back pocket and pulled it out.

"Excuse me," I said, jumping in front of the lady who was getting on the bus with three kids.

I bounced onto the bus, went to a back row, and slid down into my seat, praying and fighting back tears for my friend.

CHAPTER 39

I wanted to look out the window of the bus, but I was too scared. The bus had taken off, but I couldn't be sure if Monster's goons had seen me, so I stayed hunched down in the seat.

The woman who I'd almost knocked over getting onto the bus sat down in the seat across from me. The two smallest of her children were clutching her like she'd just returned from war. The oldest was sitting in a seat in front of them. They were all smothering her as if they didn't want to take their eyes off her.

About five minutes into the ride, they all seemed to relax. And when I peeked out the window and saw the Cutlass was long gone, I relaxed, too.

The woman and I made eye contact, and I felt compelled to say, "Sorry about almost knocking you over when we were getting on the bus."

She gave me a warm smile. "It's okay. You seemed in a bit of a hurry. Is everything okay?"

I nodded as I pulled myself up in the seat. I know I probably looked crazy all slunked down. "I'm all right."

"You know, you're about the same age as my oldest son," she told me.

"Oh," I said, not knowing what else I was supposed to say.

"That look on your face. It's one my son has when he gets into trouble." She paused and then added, "You know, God can help you find a way from trouble. He can straighten things out that you may not think can ever be worked out."

I looked at this woman like she was crazy. God didn't come to the ghetto, or else there wouldn't be a ghetto. So, the last thing I felt like hearing was any kind of sermon from her.

"Thank you, ma'am," I said simply. I might have been a "thug," but my grandmother still made sure I was raised with manners.

"No, I'm serious," the woman continued. "It might not seem like it" — she squeezed her children's hands — "but God is always working for us. In fact, He just delivered me from a situation I never thought possible."

"Okay," I said, forcing a smile and regretting that I had ever spoken to her.

"I'm just saying, when you're at your lowest, remember who can pick you up."

"Okay," I said, only this time I forgot those respectful manners my Grams had taught me and rolled my eyes.

"Mama, I'm hungry," the little boy said. I was grateful for his interruption so she could stop her preaching.

"Okay, sweetie," she said. "I'll fix you something when we get home."

I thought about those bologna sandwiches I had dropped when I was running from Monster and his goons, and my stomach instantly growled.

"Oh, you know what?" the woman said, "I have some chips and juice in my bag."

She pulled out several small bags of generic-looking Fritos. She handed each of them a bag and had just opened the bag for herself when she caught me staring. I don't know if it was the way my mouth was watering or if it was because I was looking at those chips like they were the Last Supper, but she said, "You know what? This isn't even on my diet plan. Would you like them?" She offered the bag to me.

I wanted to decline, but my stomach cursed me for even thinking about saying no.

I nodded, and she handed me the chips, along with a Capri Sun. I pulled the chips out of the bag and devoured them. Her kids were staring at me, and I realized I must have looked like some kind of savage.

"Sorry. Just a little hungry," I said, my mouth full of chips.

"It's okay," the woman replied with a warm, nonjudgmental smile.

"Mommy, do you have to go back to work?" the little girl said, not interested in anything I had going on. "The last time you went there . . ."

"I know, sweetheart. But that's not going to happen this time."

"You promise?" the little boy asked.

"I promise." She rubbed his hair.

They sulked and I got out of their conversation and returned to thoughts of what I was going to do next. I had nowhere to go. No money, and I couldn't ride this bus forever. I reached into my back pocket for my cell phone and realized it was gone. I cursed because I thought I'd dropped something when I pulled my bus pass out to get on the bus. But I'd been in such a hurry that I didn't pay it any attention. It was dead since I'd been gone from home so long, but I still needed it.

The woman reached up and pulled the string for her stop. She turned to me as they stood. "You take care of yourself, okay, young man?"

"Yes, ma'am," I replied.

She flashed one last smile and then got off the bus.

We had just taken off when I looked down and noticed the bag from which she'd pulled the snacks.

"Hey," I said, jumping up and trying to tap the window, but by that point she was gone, shuffling her children ahead of her as they walked down the street.

I fell back in my seat and glanced in the bag. There were a few envelopes, other stuff, and a black wallet.

That lady was talking about God. Maybe this was the blessing she was talking about coming my way. I glanced around the bus. There were only a few other people on it, and no one was paying any attention to me, so I leaned over and slid the bag toward me. I reached in, pulled out the wallet, and opened it, hoping to find some money. I saw pictures of her kids and my heart slowed a bit. I wondered if my mother had ever carried pictures of us. It was obvious the love that woman had for her children. The sight of those pictures in her wallet made me long for Grams. While my mom wasn't the best at mothering, Grams always made sure we knew that we were loved.

"Dang," I said when I looked through her wallet. She had eleven dollars. A ten and a one-dollar bill. That would do nothing for me. I pulled out what looked like her work badge.

"The Markham Hotel. Anna Rodríguez," I read. I stuffed it back in her bag and went through it some more. That's when I noticed what looked like some court papers and birth certificates. There was also a newspaper article with her picture, so I scanned the story.

Wow. This woman had been through it, I thought after I'd finished reading. She'd almost been deported, and like me, her kids would've been motherless. I wondered if she'd need these official-looking papers.

But it was the next thing I found in her bag that made my heart move from a slow beat to a full-on pause. It was a string of beads, I think they call them a rosary, that were wrapped around a photo. A photo of a young Hispanic guy. A photo of Paco.

You're about the same age as my oldest son.

Anna Rodríguez.

Paco Rodríguez.

This was Paco's mother!

The beads trembled in my hands. I wondered: Did she know he was dead? Had the police ID'd him and let her know? I thought about it. She couldn't know because she spoke like she thought he was still living.

Oh, my God. I needed to tell her about Paco. And I needed to get her back her bag.

"Hey, mister," I said to the bus driver once he pulled away from the next stop. "This lady left her bag."

"Throw it in this trash bin," he said without looking up at me. "I'm sick of folks leaving their mess on my bus."

I side-eyed him, then decided I'd return this to her myself. I'd done enough wrong in my life. Now I wanted to do something right. I owed Paco that much.

"Hey, do you know where the Markham Hotel is?" I asked the driver.

"Do I look like a GPS?" he snapped.

"Really, man? What is your problem?"

He slammed on the brakes. There were five other people on the bus, and all of us braced ourselves to keep from falling.

"Have you lost your mind?" I yelled.

He threw the bus in park, turned to me, and jabbed a finger in my direction. "I'm

324

sick of you little punks coming on my bus and trying to talk to me crazy."

"What are you talking about? I just asked a question," I said.

He stood and faced me. "You're a disrespectful little punk. Now, get off my bus!"

I was dumbfounded. Either this guy had had a really bad day or he was out of his mind.

He reached down, pulled the lever, and swung the door open. "Get off my bus."

"What?" I was still trying to understand what I'd done wrong.

"I said, get off."

He reached for my arm like he was going to force me off, but I jerked it away.

"Don't make me call the cops," he warned.

I couldn't believe this was happening. "Fine!"

I got off the bus, still in shock and wondering what I was supposed to do now.

Yet I knew. I'd been put off the bus so I could go find Mrs. Rodríguez and break the news about her son.

I sighed and began walking in the direction I'd seen her go.

CHAPTER 40

I had been walking for about thirty minutes. I still didn't know where I was headed. I just went back in the direction we'd come from. I knew I was near downtown, but I had no idea where I was going from here. I felt something vibrating in the bag and realized it was the lady's cell phone.

I waited for the call to stop, then decided to see if she had Internet, since this was one of the earlier iPhones. Thankfully, it wasn't locked. Tapping the Safari icon, I pulled up the address for the Markham Hotel, then used the GPS to direct me. I thought about keeping the phone, since I'd lost mine, but once she found out she'd lost it, she'd probably cut it off, so it wouldn't do me any good anyway.

I don't know why I was bothering to take this lady's bag back, but I was determined. I was just about to turn the corner when I saw a royal-blue car with what looked like

Monster's bodyguard driving. I couldn't tell for sure if it was Monster's crew, but I took off running anyway. Thankfully, as soon as I got to the next street, the Markham Hotel loomed in front of me. I darted inside, praying if that was Monster, I hadn't been spotted.

"Yes, may I help you?" the man at the front desk said as I came in.

"Yeah, ummm, ummm," I stammered, then remembered the bag. "Yeah, I found this and it belongs to one of your employees."

"Really, you *found* it?" He raised his left eyebrow. "Which employee?" I could tell he was suspicious.

"Someone named Anna Rodríguez. Her badge was in there." I looked around.

"Anna isn't here," he said.

I paused, trying to figure out my next move. "Is it okay if I just wait for her to come to work?"

"She doesn't work here anymore."

"Oh. I just assumed this is where she was headed because her kid said something about not wanting her to go to work."

"Well, I can call her. Just leave the bag with me," the man said.

I was just about to hand the bag over when Mrs. Rodríguez walked into the lobby.

"Hi, you're the young man from the bus," she said, smiling at me as she approached the counter. Her eyes went to her bag in my hand. "Is that mine?"

"H-hi, yes, ma'am." I held up the bag. "You left this at your seat."

"Oh, my God. I left it on the bus. I have been retracing my steps, thinking maybe I dropped it because I could've sworn I had it when I got off."

"Yeah, I just thought I'd bring it to you. I looked in it to get your information and thought, you know, maybe you needed the stuff in there," I said. "I didn't take nothin'," I felt the need to add.

"You have no idea," she said, surprising me as she pulled me into a bear hug. "This has my wallet, ID, my new work visa, and what little money I do have in it."

"Hmph," the guy behind the counter mumbled. "Anna, you'd better check it."

I cut my eyes at him. I didn't have the time to deal with him. I kept glancing at the door, afraid that at any moment Monster and his crew would come in.

"I wish I had money to give you for a reward," she said.

"I didn't do it for a reward," I told her. "It was the least I could do for you since, you know, you gave me the chips. The papers look really important, and I thought you might need them."

Her face took on a questioning look and she studied me. "Is everything really okay?"

"Um, yeah, yeah," I said. I was trying to get up the nerve to tell her about Paco. But how do you tell a mother her son is dead? "Well, I, ah . . . I just wanted to turn this in." I glanced nervously around, then said, "Y'all got a bathroom around here?" Maybe if I had a little time to get myself together, I could tell her about Paco.

She nodded and pointed down the hall.

I thanked her, then took off. I ducked into the bathroom wondering how long I could hide out there. After about fifteen minutes, I heard a tap on the door, then Anna stuck her head in.

"Are you okay?" she asked me again.

I wanted to lie, but I was really scared. "Not really," I admitted. "It's some guys after me."

She paused like she was wondering if she should get involved. Then she stepped into the men's bathroom. "Did you do something wrong?" she asked.

"No, I swear. But they said I owe them money and I'm just scared they're going to be waiting for me," I said.

Anna sighed, then stuck her head back

out the door. Seconds later, she reappeared. "Come with me."

I followed her out of the bathroom. She peeked toward the lobby, then dipped in the opposite direction toward the stairwell. I waited a few seconds before I followed her. I didn't ask questions as we climbed three flights of stairs.

"Wait right here," she said when we got to the third floor.

She cracked the door that led into the hallway and said, "Rosa? Rosa?"

I heard someone say, "Anna, what are you doing here?"

"I came to turn in my keys and uniform and get my check that I never picked up," she replied.

"You know I would've done that for you," she said.

"It's okay. But look, I need a favor."

The lady must have been realizing by that time that Anna was peeking out of the stairwell. Her voice sounded like it was getting closer as she said, "Why did you take the stairwell? And why are you whispering?"

Anna opened the door and I cowered behind her.

"Who is that?" the lady asked.

Anna turned to me. "What's your name, sweetie?"

"Trey," I said.

She turned back to the woman. "This is Trey."

Rosa's eyes scanned me from head to toe. "Obviously, since you're asking him his name, you don't know him, so what are you doing?"

"Rosa, Trey is in a little trouble."

"Okay, and . . . ?"

"Do you have an open room?"

Rosa cocked her head at her friend. "Really, Anna?"

Anna shrugged. "I'm already fired, so it doesn't matter. All I need is for you to answer the question, then you can go clean the fourth floor."

"Again, why are you doing this?"

"Because someone just helped me, remember?"

Rosa sighed and started what I guess she called whispering, even though I could hear her loud and clear. "How do you know he's not some kind of killer, or thug, or gangbanger?" she asked.

"I'm not," I spoke up.

She gave me the side-eye, then said, "Fine. But I don't know anything about anything."

"Which rooms are empty?"

She looked at me one last time, then said, "Ugh, 318 and 316 are empty." Rosa handed her a key card.

"Okay."

"I'm gone, I don't know anything. I never saw you." Rosa threw up her hands as she walked off. Anna motioned for me to follow her. She stopped in front of 318, but then said, "You know what, I'm going to put you in 316 because there's a book in there that might do you some good." She opened the door and walked in the room.

A book, really? I'm running for my life and this lady is talking about reading? But since I didn't want to mess up anything, I kept my mouth shut and followed her in.

"Now, you can't stay but a day."

"What if someone checks in?" I asked.

"I'm going to go downstairs and talk to Wayne, my friend at the front desk."

"He didn't like me."

"That's okay, he likes me." She smiled. "But you've got to promise me, no trouble. You can eat out of the minibar, Rosa will take care of that. I'll swing back by tomorrow and make sure everything is okay when it's time for you to leave."

"Why are you doing this?" I repeated the question her friend had just asked.

"Like I told Rosa, someone just helped me. Plus, I have a son your age, and he finds trouble himself. I pray if he ever needs help, someone will help him."

Tell her.

How was I supposed to tell this sweet woman her son was dead?

Just do it.

"Mrs. Rodríguez . . . um, I have something to tell you," I began.

"Yes?"

I couldn't do it. Me telling her about her son wasn't going to bring him back. All it would do was cause her to lose it, pass out or something, which would bring attention to my being here and I'd probably get kicked out. No, I decided. I'd tell her when she came by tomorrow.

I hugged her. "I just wanted to tell you, thank you so much."

She smiled. "No. Thank you. Not many people would've returned my bag." She walked over and closed the blinds before turning to me. "Make yourself at home, but I need you to be respectful."

"Yes, ma'am."

"Where are you going from here?" she asked.

I shrugged. "I just need to get some sleep and try to figure out my next move."

I was thankful that she didn't ask any more questions. "Okay. You know what, I can swing two days, but you'll have to leave after that. So you can stay till Thursday. For now, though, just rest." She pointed to a tattered Bible on the nightstand. "You might want to glance through that. It'll help you with whatever you're going through."

I fake-smiled as I nodded. "Yes, ma'am. I sure will."

As soon as she closed the door, I didn't give that book a second thought. I turned on the TV and started flipping the channels, looking for BET.

CHAPTER 41

This was the life.

Now I could see why people got caught up in making money because if money could provide like this, I definitely wanted it. The problem was, I wanted mine legally.

Getting it Monster's way meant you were always running in fear, and I was tired of running. I had visions of me and Jamal traveling the world, chillin' in hotels like this. We'd never been anywhere really. We went to Galveston once when I was a little boy, but other than that, we'd never been outside of the Houston area.

I'd had the best night's sleep in years. The mattress was everything, and I'd never slept under such a plush bedspread.

The shower was next. At Gram's and Ms. Laura's, the water was always trickling and was always either too hot or too cold. This shower had been perfect.

Being still had given me a moment to

reflect on the last couple of days. I cried for my friends and finally had to push thoughts of them aside or I'd never be able to figure out my next move.

I flipped the channels, seeing what was on TV. I stopped at *The Fresh Prince of Bel-Air.* That was one of my favorite shows. Maybe because I dreamed of being whisked away to a different world.

I'd just laughed at some antic from Will Smith when the show went to a commercial break. The pretty young girl that appeared caught my eye. She was sitting on a plush lawn reading a book as a narrator talked over her.

"When the world is your oyster, let Jarvis Christian College arm you with the tools to succeed," the voice said.

It was a shot of a small campus, and my heart immediately ached as I thought of Wiz. I wondered if he'd even have a funeral since there was no one to plan one. Maybe if I hadn't talked Wiz out of running, he would still be here and fulfilling his dream of going to college. The thought made the ache in my heart throb.

"Come to Jarvis Christian College, where a whole new world awaits you," the narrator continued.

The commercial reminded me that I

needed to call Mr. G. from the Boys & Girls Club. He was the only person that could get me details on Wiz. And maybe he could tell Mrs. Rodríguez about Paco so I wouldn't have to. I picked up the phone and dialed the club. I only remembered the number because it had been the same for as long as I'd attended the Boys & Girls Club.

"Hi, Mr. G., it's Trey," I said after the receptionist patched me through.

"Hey, man." He sounded genuinely happy to hear from me. "How are you holding up? I heard about Wiz."

"I'm okay," I said.

"Word on the street is Monster's crew took him out?"

I was silent. The last thing I was about to do was snitch on Monster. I was in enough trouble as it was. I wanted to ask him if he knew about Paco, but since he hadn't said anything about him, I could only assume he didn't know.

Mr. G. took my silence as my answer and said, "I hate that you're caught up in all of this, Trey."

"Yeah, me too." Silence filled the phone again. "Have you heard anything about Wiz's funeral?"

"Naw. I checked. Heard they were going to be taking him to County. There probably won't be a funeral."

Another pain shot through my chest. My man couldn't even be properly laid to rest.

"Wiz told me about you getting him into Jarvis," I said, trying to change the subject and get my mind off Wiz.

"Yep, it makes me sad because they'd given us the scholarship to disburse and Wiz was so excited." Mr. G. paused, then said, "What about you?"

"What about me?"

"I told Wiz I wanted to talk about getting you both in school there."

"Me? Man, you know I ain't no college material."

"No. I know you *are* college material. You're the one who doesn't know you're college material."

For the first time since Wiz had brought up college, I wondered . . . could this be my out, too? Just as quickly as the thought came, it was gone.

"Nah, you know about my little brother," I said. "He's in the system and I gotta stay around so I can make sure they don't abuse him or anything."

"Well, until you get your life together, you can't be any good to him. And the only way you can get it together is to get out of the game."

338

He had that right. "You know this ain't me. I don't even like the game," I said.

"That's my point exactly. That's why it may be time to try something different. That's what I told Wiz."

I finally stopped to think about it. I'd been saving money because my dream was to get out of this life, but I didn't really have a plan. A college degree could be a plan. Jamal would be twelve or thirteen by the time I finished, but that would be enough time for me to make an impact in his life. If I had a college degree, a decent job, and some money, no way could a social worker deny me getting my brother. "You really think I could make it in college?"

"I know you could," he replied. He sounded like he was getting excited that I would actually consider it. "And me and the other counselors would be there to help you."

"What about Jamal?" I asked. "You know I can't leave him."

"I'll check on Jamal, and every time you come home you can go see him."

I knew Mr. G. was right. Not only was I in no position to take care of Jamal, once Monster found me I wouldn't even be around to take care of him.

"You know, I just may take you up on

that," I finally said.

"Great! You should come by here tomorrow so we can talk this out."

I had to let him know the situation. "I'm kinda on the run."

"Where are you now?" he asked without hesitation. That's why we all liked him — he never judged us.

"I'm at some hotel downtown." I glanced at the name on the phone. "The Markham Hotel is the name. But I can only stay here through tomorrow."

He went quiet like he was thinking. "I would let you stay here, but I can't bring that Monster drama to my doorstep. We recently adopted a little boy and I can't put him in any danger."

"Nah, I'm good, Mr. G. I wouldn't do that to you. And congrats on your son."

"Thanks." He paused like he was deep in thought. "You know what? Here's what I can do," he continued. "I'll call the social worker, see if we can do a day pass visit, and I'll bring Jamal to see you."

That brought an instant smile to my face. "For real?"

"Yeah. I'll also make some calls about the college. I have all your high school stuff on file. I've seen your grades, so I know you can do this. Switching the application from

William — I mean Wiz — to you shouldn't be a problem. Then we'll put you on a bus."

"I don't have anything — clothes, shoes, nothing."

"Do you need to go by your house?"

I thought about the two raggedy pairs of tennis shoes I had. The one decent pair of Jordans that I'd splurged on from Monster's money were on my feet. And my closet was bare. No, I didn't need to risk going back to Ms. Laura's for those few things.

"Nah. You think you can get me some clothes?"

"Of course, you're what, a thirty-two and a large?"

"Yes," I said, surprised that he knew, since I hadn't been to see him in months.

"Great, we'll bring you some clothes and toiletries tomorrow," he said.

"So I would leave now?" This was not what I'd envisioned when I'd called him.

"Didn't you say you're running from Monster?"

This was all moving so fast. "Yeah, but . . . just wow. I don't even know where Jarvis is."

"It's right outside Dallas," he said.

"What am I going to do once I get there?"

"Don't worry, you can work through the end of the year. We'll hook you up with my contact there, and you can start school in January. Trust me, we'll work it all out."

I couldn't believe this. Going to college had been the last thing I'd expected when I picked up the phone to call.

"Just hang tight. Lay low tonight, and I'll come by tomorrow at noon. Meet me in the lobby. Cool?"

I smiled. "Cool." Then I added, "Mr. G., thank you so much."

"It's my pleasure. You know it's my life's work to help you guys out," he said before hanging up.

I leaned back against the headboard.

I was going to college.

Maybe I'd do like Wiz said, join a fraternity, meet a nice college girl, and most of all, get an education that opened the door to a better life. I looked around the room. That opened the door to *this* life.

I glanced over at that book. I hadn't cracked it open, but I was grateful that whatever was in there had led Mrs. Rodríguez to want to help me. Otherwise, I would've never seen the Jarvis commercial and I wouldn't have called Mr. G.

My grandmother used to always say there are angels in our midst. My angels — Mrs. Rodríguez and Mr. G. — had just put my future on a whole new path.

CHAPTER 42

"Trey!"

The sight of my little brother running toward me made my heart swell with joy. He jumped into my arms and I swung him around.

"Look at you, you little knucklehead!" I said, palming his forehead.

"I don't have a knucklehead!"

"Yes, you do," I said. "But it's the best-looking knucklehead I've ever seen." I hugged him tightly as I looked up at Mr. G., standing beside us in the lobby of the Markham Hotel. "Thank you so much," I mouthed.

Mr. G. nodded. "We had to work some magic, but God must've been on your side." He winked, and then I noticed the pretty lady standing next to him.

"Hello," I said.

"Hi," she replied.

"This is my wife, Savannah," Mr. G. said.

"Babe, this is Trey, Jamal's brother that I was telling you about. You met him years ago, back when he used to come to the Boys & Girls Club all the time."

"How are you? Yes, you have definitely grown up from the last time I saw you," she said.

"I'm great now that I got to see my little brother." I hugged Jamal again.

"Can we go play basketball?" Jamal asked.

"I wish."

Mr. G. knelt down so that he was face-to-face with my little brother.

"Jamal, remember I told you. We are just here to see your brother for a little bit."

Jamal buried his face in my shoulder. "I wanna stay with him."

That almost made me cry.

"You know what, Jamal? You see that candy over there by the front desk? How would you feel about some Skittles?" Mr. G. asked as he stood.

The mention of Skittles must have made Jamal forget what he was just upset about, because he jumped up and down. "Yes!"

Mr. G. handed him two dollars and pointed to the counter. "Just tell that man over there what you want and he'll get it. We'll be standing right here. I'm not taking my eyes off you."

I watched him dart over to the counter, and reality started to set in.

"I don't know how I'm going to make it at school worried about him. I've heard horror stories about those group homes. At least with me going every other day, I could check on him."

Mr. G. and his wife exchanged looks. "Are you thinking what I'm thinking?" he asked her.

She nodded. They were smiling at each other like they were up to no good. "Frankie would love a sibling," she said.

"What are you guys talking about?" I asked. "Who's Frankie?"

"The little boy who I told you my wife and I just adopted," Mr. G. said. "He just came home last week and we're already in love. He's in school right now."

"Oh, cool," I said. A thought came to me, and a quick pang shot through my heart. I didn't want Jamal to get adopted because I was coming back to get him, but I did want him to go to a safe foster home. But what if he got with a family that didn't let him see me?

"Franklin is seven," Mr. G. said, "close in age to Jamal."

Now I was wondering what they were talking about.

"And well," Mrs. G. spoke up, "we were thinking Franklin might like a big brother."

"What?" I said.

"Well, my wife and I kinda bonded with Jamal on the way over here," Mr. G. said. "And once she learned he's in the system . . ."

Mrs. G. continued his sentence. "I knew immediately that I'd like to get to know your brother a little better. And then maybe he can come live with us. That way you can see him whenever you want," she said. "We're already certified so we'd make excellent foster parents."

I looked back and forth between them.

"Are you serious, Mr. G.?"

"As triple bypass surgery," he replied. "I figured you'd be able to focus on school if you know your little brother is well taken care of."

I wanted to jump for joy right there in that hotel lobby.

"Oh, snap. That's awesome," I said. I was hugging both of them when Mrs. Rodríguez walked into the lobby.

"Mrs. Rodríguez," I called out to her. I knew she was coming to make sure I got out of the room okay. "Over here!" She headed over to me.

"Hello, Trey. How was everything?" Some-

346

thing was different about her. Her eyes were reddish and her smile didn't seem as genuine as it was the other day. Still, I couldn't contain my excitement.

"You were right!" I exclaimed. "Everything worked out."

I threw my arms around her neck, too, which caught her by surprise. "Well, that's some kind of thank-you. I guess that means your room was fine?"

"It was better than fine, and I didn't even eat everything out of the minibar!"

She laughed, then noticed Mrs. G. "Savannah? What in the world are you doing here?"

She looked surprised as well. "Actually, we're here for Trey. But I thought you were working with the Freedom Coalition," she said.

"I am," Mrs. Rodríguez replied. "I just came to make sure Trey was okay. You know him?"

"Yes, he's one of the kids in my husband's program."

"Well, small world." Mrs. Rodríguez smiled, then looked at Mr. G. in recognition. "Aren't you from the Boys & Girls Club?"

Mr. G. nodded.

"I used to bring my son there."

"Who's your son?" Mr. G. asked.

My muscles tightened in my stomach.

Her mood turned somber. "Paco Rod-ríguez."

"Yes, Paco," Mr. G. said. "I haven't talked to him in a couple of years, how is he?"

She swallowed like she was trying to compose herself. "Unfortunately, I found out yesterday that he was killed. I was coming to see about Trey, and then —" She paused to compose herself. "I have to go to the morgue. My son has apparently been there for days."

Mr. and Mrs. G. gasped. I looked away.

"I am so sorry," Mrs. G. said. Mr. G. was studying me and I could tell he knew I knew something.

"I have cried all night," Mrs. Rodríguez continued, "but I know God has His reasons for everything." She took a deep breath, then managed a faint smile. "Just pray for my family's strength. My children are not taking this well."

"Of course," Mrs. G. said.

Her eyes must've asked an unspoken question because Mrs. Rodríguez said, "I have no idea what Paco's death means for me, but I just have to stay faithful."

Mrs. G. squeezed her hand. "Keep in touch and let me know if there is anything we can do."

Jamal came running back up to us. He held up his bag. "I got Tropical Skittles," he announced.

"May I have some?" I asked, if for no other reason than to ease the heavy cloud that hung over us.

Jamal looked around at all of us. "Okay, everybody gets two." I couldn't help but smile because he was serious.

"I say we go grab some dinner, then take you to the bus station," Mr. G. said after my brother had distributed his Skittles.

"Oh, you're leaving?" Mrs. Rodríguez said.

I nodded. "Going to start a new life. Thank you for saving my old one."

"I'm so glad our paths crossed." Now, her smile was genuine.

She reached in and hugged me. "I couldn't save my son." She patted my cheek. "But I'm grateful I could help save you. I need to get going, though." Fresh tears sprung to her eyes. "I have a funeral to plan."

I felt guilty that I hadn't told her what I knew about Paco or that I even knew him. But it was obvious that she'd been through enough. And I had no doubt that she had the strength to carry on.

"Take care of yourself," Mrs. G. said, hugging her. "And again, let me know if you need anything."

Mrs. Rodríguez managed one last smile before she walked away.

We all looked down at Jamal, who was intensely studying each Skittle, and that lightened the mood.

"Come on," I said, reaching for my brother's hand. "Let's roll, li'l bro."

As we left out of the Markham Hotel, Jamal's hand intertwined with mine, and with Mr. and Mrs. G. close behind us, it felt like . . . a family. I knew we weren't a family. But after what Mr. G. and his wife were doing for me, I couldn't help but feel like we were destined to be one.

It's amazing how just a matter of days, in one room, could change the course of someone's life.

I was grateful that someone was me and for the first time in my young life, I felt hope.

A NOTE FROM THE AUTHOR

When you've written forty-plus books, you'd think that you might run out of ideas. But the universe has been kind to me, by giving me an infinite amount of creativity. (Okay, and some drama-filled family and friends that keep me swathed in story ideas.) I am just thankful that I am able to continue to create books that people want to read.

I wake up every day thanking God for that blessing.

I've lost count of which book number this actually is. I don't know if that's a good thing or a bad thing. But I've been blessed to have a long and somewhat successful career doing what I love. I wouldn't be able to do what I love were it not for all the people in my corner.

Thank you to my amazing family. Though you long ago stopped being impressed with my new books, your support has never wavered. To my children — I love you to the moon and beyond. Special shout-out to my little sissy, Tanisha Tate. Y'all, I love this chick. The end.

My business partner, writing partner, therapist, voice of reason, and friend-till-the-end, Victoria Christopher Murray, thank you for always helping me talk through my stories, for picking up the slack when I'm slacking, for providing motivation and encouragement, and for getting me off the couch . . . I am eternally grateful.

My core . . . my forever ride-or-die friends who stopped reading at book number two but never stopped supporting — Jaimi Canady, Raquelle Lewis, Kim Wright, and Clemelia Humphrey Richardson — love you ladies for life!

Pat Tucker, I am forever grateful for your support and friendship. Nina Foxx, I'm blessed to call you a friend.

To my soror, my friend, my publicist, Norma Warren, who will never admit it, but I'm sure has called me some very unsisterly names☺, thank you for your love and patience. I'm still working to #DoBetter.

To my BGB admin family: Jason, Cherritta, Kimyatta, Raine . . . thank you so much for all that you do. To our amazing partners . . . I'm thrilled to have you on our team.

As usual, thanks to my agent since day one, Sara Camilli; my editor from the beginning, Brigitte Smith, and my new editor, Marla Daniels; my wonderful publicist, Melissa Gramstad; and the rest of my family at Gallery. Thank you for continuously believing in me!

Editor extraordinaire John Paine, once again you worked your magic. My books soar because of you.

Thank you to some very special friends who helped my muse be her best on this book: Jay, Dishan, Eddie, James, Jihad, and my cousin, Moses.

A thousand thanks to my literary colleagues: Da Bad Authoresses, Tiffany Warren, Renee Flagler (you guys make this literary journey bearable☺), Eric Jerome Dickey, Stacey Evans Morgan, Brian Smith, Victor McGlothin, Kwame Alexander, Karla Bady, and Kimberla Lawson Roby. Special shout-outs to: Monique S. Hall, Sharon Lucas, Yolanda Gore, Cecie Reed, Sophie Sealy, Nakecia Bowers, Eric Jamal, Sheretta Edwards, Lisa Paige Jones, Tres Dunmore, April Moore Gipson, Bridget Crawford, King Brooks, Tiffany Tyler, Lisa Meade Hawkins, Gina Torres, Michelle Chavis, Michelle Harden, Shawn Rushing, Pam Gaskin, Radiah Hubert, Lynn Clouser,

Orsayor Simmons, and my sister-cousin, Shay Smith.

I could list book clubs for days. But I want to give a special acknowledgment to A Novel Idea, Brownstone Book Club, Sistahs in Conversation and Sistahs in Harmony, Black Butterfly, Cover 2 Cover, Savvy, Nubian Pageturners, Cush City, Black Pearls Keepin It Real, Mahogany, Women of Substance, My Sisters & Me, Pages Between Sistahs, Shared Thoughts, Brag About Books, Mocha Readers, Characters, Christian Fiction Café, Sisters Who Like to Read, Readers of Delight, Tabahani Book Circle, FB Page Turners, African-American Women's Book Club, Women of Color, Zion M.B.C. Women's Book Club, Jus'Us, Go On Girl Texas 1, Book Club Etc., Pearls of Wisdom, Renaissance, Lady Lotus, and Soulful Readers of Detroit, Brownstone (please know that if you're not here, it doesn't diminish my gratitude).

Thank you to all the wonderful libraries that have also supported my books, introduced me to readers, and fought to get my books on the shelves.

People often ask why I take time to thank my Facebook friends. But I've gotten so much love, encouragement, and support from my social media family. While I'm sure

I'm missing someone, thank you to: Bernice, Allison, J'son, Natalie, Davina, Kiera, Rachel, Bettye, Ronnesha, Karen, Natalie, Sonja, Lisa, Lateefah, Gail, Juda, Ingrid, Vicki, Shelly, Charlene, Michelle, Karla, Tracey, Karyn, Crystal, Eddgra, Tonia, Kimberlee, Cindy, Annette, Nicole, Chenoa, Brenda, JE, Tanisha, Beverly, Noelle, Kim, Princis, Joe, Charlenette, Yasmin, Terri, Cheryl, Kelley, Katharyn, Bridget, Alicia, Arnesha, Tamou, Sharmel, Antoinette, Cynthia, Jackie, Ernest, Wanda, Ralph, Patrick, Lissha, Tameka, Laura, Marsha, Wanda, Kym, Allison, Jacole, Stephanie, Dawn, Paula, Nakia, Jodi, Cecily, Leslie, Gary, Cryssy, KP, Tomaiya, Gwen, Nik, Martha, Joyce, Yolanda, Lasheera. (Y'all know I could go on and on . . .)

Lots of love and gratitude to my sorors of Alpha Kappa Alpha Sorority, Inc. (including my own chapter, Mu Kappa Omega); our illustrious president, Dorothy Buckhanan Wilson; my sisters in Greekdom, Delta Sigma Theta Sorority, Inc., who *constantly* show me love . . . and my fellow mothers in Jack and Jill of America, Inc., especially the Missouri City–Sugar Land and Durham Chapters.

And finally, thanks to YOU . . . my beloved reader. If it's your first time picking up one of my books, I truly hope you enjoy. If you're coming back, words cannot even begin to express how eternally grateful I am for your support. From the bottom of my heart, thank you!

Much Love,
ReShonda

ABOUT THE AUTHOR

ReShonda Tate Billingsley's #1 national bestselling novels include *Let the Church Say Amen, I Know I've Been Changed,* and *Say Amen, Again,* winner of the NAACP Image Award for Outstanding Literary Work. Her collaboration with Victoria Christopher Murray has produced four hit novels, *Sinners & Saints, Friends & Foes, A Blessing and a Curse,* and *Fortune & Fame.* BET released a movie in 2013 based on ReShonda's book *Let the Church Say Amen* in which she had a minor role. She also had a role in the made-for-TV movie *The Secret She Kept* based on her book of the same title. Visit ReShondaTateBillingsley.com, meet the author on Facebook at ReShon daTateBillingsley, or follow her on Twitter @Reshondat.